HERE COMES THE BRIDE

ctor Headley lives and works in London
and Jamaica.
ere Comes The Bride is his fifth ovel.

Also by Victor Headley

YARDIE
EXCESS
YUSH
FETISH

Victor Headley

HERE COMES THE BRIDE

The
X
Press

Published by
The X Press, 6 Hoxton Square, London N1 6NU
Tel: 0171 729 1199   Fax: 0171 729 1771

Distributed by Turnaround, Unit 3, Olympia Trading Estate, Coburg
Road, London N22 6TZ
Tel: 0181 829 3000   Fax: 0181 881 5088

Printed by Caledonian International Book Manufacturing Ltd,
Glasgow, UK

ISBN   1-874509-36-0

This tale is for my children; 'You make it all worthwhile!'

•T H E   C O U N T D O W N•

...*Apart from all these impressive qualifications and rare skills, I also have an amazingly warm and instantly lovable personality. I can hear you rightly say: "Fine, fine, but what have you been doing these past three years? Your records of employment stop in June of '93..." Well, sir... or madam, these last three years have been the most wonderful of all my life. I have learned the ways of the world, using the only method there is — going on the road. I am proud to tell you that in less than thirty-six months I have visited, and in some cases lived in, thirteen countries, ranging as far afield as India and Sweden. I cannot begin to tell you the stories from these travels, but I am sure you will appreciate the richness of experience a person like myself could bring to a company such as yours.*

I remain at your disposal, should you require any further details about me or my past activities and experience.

Faithfully yours,
M.

With a little grin, Mo saved the document and hit the "print" button on the PC. That might just do it, he thought.

If he was going to apply for jobs, he might as well hit them with a CV that differed sharply from the piles of them these executives went though every day. 'Cause this was no ordinary CV, and it came from no ordinary applicant! For any company to have the privilege of receiving a job application from the great Mo and not respond favourably was unimaginable. That's the way Mo saw it, anyway.

But in truth, the way Mo really saw it wasn't that clear-cut at all. "Do I really want a job?" he kept asking himself. He realised it this morning, while pulling his CV and covering letter out of the printer in his local library: he was starting to do things out of compulsion.

No, Mo didn't really really want a job — not the kind of job he was applying for, in any case. But because it seemed to be the right thing to do, he was doing it. The few grand he had in his building society account could see him through for a while; he'd been looking around to see where he could invest that money. As a man who was used to being his own boss, it was going to be hard holding a regular job, he knew that much. And besides, no job was going to pay him as much as he was used to earning. So why in the world was he sweating over these application forms?

2

He knew he had been doing things over the last three months that had nothing to do with what he wanted, but he'd been doing them anyway. Or rather, he had been going along with decisions taken by someone else. Why? Well, because that was the way he had told himself he should act now — responsibly. That was the new Mo, and he had stuck to his new image. So far.

So why was he thinking like this today? Mo checked himself, held back his train of thoughts and shook his head to clear it up. Across the large study table he caught a glimpse of a smile on someone's face. It sunk behind the big atlas so quickly that Mo couldn't be sure he'd seen it at all.

He had been muttering to himself unawares; that was a bad sign! Picking up his notebook and pen, he went to pay for his prints and left the library.

"What a difference a day makes" the song goes, and it's all true. Walking up the sunny high street, totally oblivious to the lunch-hour activity around him, Mo was playing back in his mind the events of the previous evening. He didn't believe in coincidences, so it must have been meant for he and Merle to meet again — and their conversation had sure made an impact on him. See how funny life is?

When he'd got home out of the pouring rain and found Nicole involved in a lively argument

3

with her ten-year-old brother, Mo hadn't paid too much attention to it at first. Since they'd both answered "Nothing" to his "What's happening?", he'd gone into the bedroom to change his clothes and prepare for an evening with a stack of newspapers and magazines he'd brought home. It was when he overheard Nicole telling her brother he would go to prison that Mo decided something serious was involved, and that he should investigate what the dispute was about.

The look on Vinny's face was pure, cold anger. Sighing, Mo sat both children down on the bed and asked again: "OK, who wants to tell me the story?"

Vinny was staring at the floor, the jaws on his youthful face clenched tight. Mo turned to Nicole. For a few seconds she seemed torn between her loyalty to her brother and her duty to her father — but this was an important matter.

"Some boys stole Vinny's bike."

Mo frowned, waited.

Nicole knew her father liked to hear all the facts, so she went on: "There was two of them, they had a knife." She stopped to observe Mo's reaction, her arched eyebrows almost meeting above the bridge of her nose in a line of concentration. She glanced briefly at her brother, who still seemed too angry to speak.

"Where was this?" Mo asked her.

"Near the shopping centre."

4

Mo sighed deeply. How could something like that take place in broad daylight on a busy street? The boys, Vinny had told Nicole, were older than him by a couple of years. Budding gangsters, apparently.

"So what were you arguing about?"

Nicole paused. One thing about his daughter, Mo thought, she didn't know how to lie, and never tried. He caught himself staring at the pretty brown face. But for his darker complexion, the young girl's features so closely mirrored his own that he was still amazed by it.

"I was trying to stop him from taking out a kitchen knife."

"A kitchen knife!" Mo repeated incredulously. He shook his head. What was happening to these kids nowadays? "D'you know the boys, Vin?" he asked.

Vinny nodded.

"D'you know where they live?"

The boy looked up at his father for the first time. "One of them lives on the estate behind the youth centre."

So Mo had put some clothes back on and they'd gone, in the beating rain, to look for the robbers. He'd tried to convince Nicole that she should wait at home for her mother to return from work, but she'd insisted on coming along.

The red-brick, four-storey buildings of the estate had looked even more drab than usual under the dark skies. Vinny knew which block

5

one of the boys lived in, but since each floor had six or seven flats, he also knew they needed to get better information. Mo knew the estate well enough; he'd spent his childhood years running around these alleys and corridors with his little gang of hoodlums. In fact, he remembered one particular door he used to knock on quite regularly, years later, back in the days... Might as well try that. They'd climbed to the third floor, Mo leading the way to the last door at the far corner of the landing.

A couple of knocks got the door unlocked from inside. The woman was well-built, of average height, with bright eyes that opened wide as she realised who the visitor was.

"Hi, Merle," Mo said.

"Oh my God! Mo? I can't believe this; when did you come back?"

Mo smiled. "A couple of months now. How you doing?"

The woman was still staring at him in wonder. "I'm fine. What about you? Jesus, I'm shocked to see you... Come in, come in."

Merle led them through to her living room, had them sit down. With one hand she was trying to smooth down the short strands of her hair, but they stood back rebelliously. Above the mantelpiece hung a picture of a crucified blond white man. From a silver frame on top of the TV, Bernard smiled in his school uniform.

"You know the children," Mo said, noticing Merle looking hard at Nicole and Vinny.

"Yes! I haven't seen them in a while. Hi, Nicole. You got so big!" She sat down opposite them and turned to Mo. "That's your son?"

"Yeah, that's Vinny."

Merle's large eyes were beaming. "Would you like a hot drink? You look all wet..."

"No, thanks. "

Mo could feel the depth of Merle's gaze. She smiled again. "The beard suits you. It makes you look older, though..."

"Yeah, I am older," Mo remarked, and before the conversation could move on any further he said, "Maybe you can help me, Merle. I'm looking for some boys who took Vinny's bike. He says one of them lives in this block."

"I know most people on this estate... What's his name?" She was looking at Vinny.

"They call him Bud," he answered, still sounding upset.

Mo thought he noticed Merle's eyes narrowing somewhat. "Excuse me a minute," she said, and reached out for the telephone.

Mo watched her dial.

"Eileen... yeah. Lincoln there?... Send both of them to me, I have something to ask them... All right, later." She put down the receiver.

"Eileen's still living here as well?" Mo asked.

"Oh yeah, we never left the area. She got her flat across the road after she had her daughter; I

7

kept this one when Mum went back to Trinidad. So, where have you been? You just... disappeared."

"It was the best thing to do at the time. I went on a world tour."

"Really?" Merle seemed very interested to learn more, but there was a knock on the door and she stood up and said, "Excuse me, Mo."

She left the room, returning a moment later followed by two boys in hooded jackets dripping with rain. The tallest one Mo didn't quite recognise, but the other was the dead stamp of his mother.

"That's Bernard?" Mo exclaimed.

"It's them!" Vinny said, standing up suddenly. But for Mo's quick grab at him, the boy would have literally jumped on the nearest of the two.

"You sure, Vinny?" Merle asked sternly.

"It's them! They stole my bike," Vinny growled. "That one had a knife!"

Merle was facing the two boys. Neither of them had said a word since entering the room. Eyes lowered, hands hanging down at their sides, they stood silently on the living room carpet. They didn't look much like highway robbers.

Vinny still seemed eager to be given a chance to unleash his fury on them; the fact they both had a couple of years and a few inches' height on him didn't seem to matter. But it wasn't to be.

"Lord gimme strength..." Merle said quietly. Her eyes had lost that candid glow. Mo watched her take a few steps to the living room door, pick up something he couldn't see from behind it. The boys knew what it was, because they both started to move towards the other end of the room.

"Don't even move," Merle said. She turned, glaring at her son and nephew, the length of rubber pipe in her hand casually hanging down. Vinny had sat back down.

"Take off your coats," the woman ordered, her voice not noticeably changed.

The look of fear on both boys' faces was unmistakable.

"So, you turn criminal now!" Merle commented sadly. Then, without any further warning, the first of the licks from the rubber pipe reached Bernard, or Bud to his friends, on the side of his face. He cried out and tried to cover up, but the second blow struck him full on his upper leg. As the rubber pipe swung back again, Merle's nephew felt the heat of the slap on his head. He didn't anticipate the second one, which hit him right on the same spot. Then Bud howled with pain as the flexible weapon smashed the hand with which he was covering his head.

As Mo watched the punishment, he noted that Merle was an impartial judge — or executioner, as it were: the two boys were receiving the same amount of blows. In fact she seemed quite experienced at this, skilful as a Shaolin fighter monk, striking high, then low, getting through to the boys' vulnerable areas despite their frantic attempts to cover up. Trapped between the wall behind them and the settee to their left, Bud and his cousin were crying unashamedly, rubbing their bruises.

Merle stopped swinging the pipe for a moment. "So you carry knife now, eh? You is a bad man!" she yelled at her son. As if the thought of it revived her ardour, she delivered five extra licks to the unfortunate would-be knifeman. Then she said simply, "Go and clean up yourself, then come back here."

Calmly, as if she just had a pleasant conversation rather than meted out physical punishment, Merle put the pipe back in its place and sat down. Nicole and Vinny were still under the shock of witnessing the harsh beating.

Even Mo, who had taken his share of corporal punishment in his time, was impressed. "I'm really glad me and you never had a fight, Merle," he said jokingly.

"I'm really sorry, Mo; I feel so embarrassed."

"It's OK. It's not your fault — that's the way these kids grow nowadays."

Merle leaned back in the chair, shook her head. "I really did try my best to raise him good, you know. It hasn't been easy since his daddy died, but I did everything I could to show him right from wrong. I know it's hard for young boys to keep straight nowadays. I talk to him, take him to church, make sure I follow his school work, but... What more can I do?"

Mo could see that, under her calm exterior, Merle really worried about her son.

The culprits reappeared, shaken but cleaned up. They weren't looking at anyone in the room.

"Right. What happened to the bike?"

There was a silence, then Lincoln said meekly, "We gave it to somebody to sell..."

Merle sighed and looked despairingly at Mo. "Twelve years old..." she said, then turned back to the boys. "You listen to me. I want you to find this bicycle right now, and give it back to Vinny. And don't come back here with no story, or else, God help me, I'm gonna send both of you to hospital tonight. You understand, Bernard?"

"Yes, Mum."

"And you know you're gonna get another beating once your mother finds out, Lincoln?"

"Yes, Auntie."

Vinny got up to go with them, insisting that he was going for his bike, so Mo sent Nicole along too. She might just be needed to restrain Vinny from the urge to fight the already battered boys. The rain had stopped and darkness was starting to drown the town. Mo wondered whether he should go with them, but Merle reassured him they would be all right.

"So, are you gonna stay around now that you're back? What are your plans, Mo?" Merle asked once they were alone.

She had switched on the TV and insisted on making him a cup of tea. Though he didn't like

11

tea, Mo sipped it all the same. Despite the unfortunate circumstances, Merle seemed so happy to see him.

"Well, I'm staying around. I have a couple of things I'd like to try, maybe set up something again..."

"Yeah? Still in the jewellery business?" Mo smiled.

"No, I'm done with that."

"Where are you staying now?"

Mo paused a while. Merle's eyes were questioning his. "I'm by Julie's," he said finally.

Merle seemed amazed. "You're back with her? After all that!"

Mo nodded, suddenly feeling all the uncertainties he had been repressing for weeks. He said, "We're getting married."

That news widened Merle's already large eyes. "You're joking!"

But she could see he wasn't. There was a silence between them for a moment. Right then, Mo knew he had in his mind a lot of unanswered questions that he had been running from but which he should really face up to very soon. "It's time I should settle down, I think," he said, aware that he didn't sound either convincing or convinced.

"It's not really my business, Mo, and I wouldn't want you to get the wrong idea, but... you sure you know what you're doing?"

Mo sighed. He wouldn't normally have concerned himself with someone else's opinion about his personal life — nowadays even less than before — but this was Merle, his old-time girlfriend, and one who had stayed close to him as a confidante through the years, always loyal and helpful if he needed her, even though he had unceremoniously dumped her when he met Julie.

He raised his hands in a fatalistic gesture. "We're all getting big, Merle..." he said, wishing she would stop scrutinising him in that way. Then he added, "I'm just trying to do the right thing."

The news came on the screen then, and the latest disaster and death stories drew both their attention for a while. Then the doorbell rang, and Merle got up to answer it.

Vinny came in first, his dignified smirk telling Mo he'd gotten back his property. The two rascals disappeared in the bedroom and Mo stood up to take his leave.

"I hope you'll keep in touch," Merle told him as she saw them to the door.

"You know I will."

"It's real nice to see you," Merle said, then she quickly raised herself to his level and gave him a little peck on the cheek.

"You take care of yourself, all right?"

"You too, Mo. Bye, Nicole. Bye, Vinny."

The children said goodbye. On the way back home, as Vinny rode ahead, Nicole asked, "She was your girlfriend, wasn't she?"

13

Mo looked at his twelve-year-old daughter. Having been away from her for five years, he had found her so grown up, so wise to many things, that he often forgot she wasn't even a teenager yet.

"Why d'you say that?"

Nicole laughed. "I'm a woman too; I can tell."

"Oh, you're a woman now!" he quipped. "What else can you tell?"

They walked on, joking and jostling. Then the rain started again and they jogged the rest of the way.

As he boarded a bus to Islington, Mo realised that his conversation with Merle the night before wasn't the reason he felt so troubled this morning; it was her reaction to his news which was now forcing him to re-evaluate everything soberly.

Questions had been brewing inside him for a while, but he had kept them from bugging him, so far, by justifying to himself his chosen course of action. This is the right thing to do, he would tell himself. But this morning that motto somehow didn't seem so solid. The right thing for whom? Why was it that suddenly those reasons he had so single-mindedly stuck to these past three months weren't enough to give him peace any more? Sure, he had willingly agreed to this marriage and, yes, he had committed himself to settle down and face his responsibilities. Yet, for all the mental conditioning he had put himself through since his return to London, he couldn't deny the disquiet he could feel rumbling deep in his soul.

The bus conductor interrupted his meditation. Whatever doubts Mo had would have to be dealt with within the next twenty-five days. After that, it would be 'till death do us part', as the pastor always declares on the day...

15

•ITS A FAMILY AFFAIR•

"Turn down this damn noise, boy!"

Vinny frowned. The high-pitched shout of his grandmother from the kitchen had interrupted his daydreaming. Grudgingly, he switched off the stereo and took out his cassette. All he wanted was to be left in peace with his music, his video games and his comic magazine, but somehow there was always someone to frustrate him.

He didn't even want to be here in the first place. He didn't like his grandmother's house, couldn't stand the place at all. The old woman wouldn't leave him alone. When he had finally grown too big for the hugs and kisses she used to smother him with, she still managed to try to control everything he did, force him to eat things he didn't like, and generally bother him constantly. No, he had no love for this house, and yet his mother had this habit of leaving him here. As far back as he could recall, he always ended up here.

Outside wasn't too bright; it looked like it might even start to rain again, like it had for most

16

of that August. But anywhere, Vinny reflected, would be better than here. Just because you're only ten doesn't mean you have to be told what to do all the time, where to go and where not to go. Imagine spending a whole Saturday morning dragged through the market, the supermarket and the stores by two excited women! It was bad enough to miss all the kids' programmes on TV, but on top of that — and this was to him the most upsetting thing — he'd had to suffer the indignity of trying on suits in no less than four different clothes shops, standing in front of mirrors, hearing all the idiotic comments of more women as he stood there wearing that stupid white shirt and bow tie.

Vinny had just about had enough of this whole wedding business anyway. The entire thing was just one distress after another for him. Perhaps the worst thing about it was the very real prospect of having to get his hair cut. He had felt quite good in the last few months with the crown of short locks atop his head, and no less than three girls at school had complimented him on it. At ten years of age, things like that mean a lot! His mother and (especially) his grandmother had strongly objected to his chosen hairstyle, but he had received Mo's full support — and that had made all the difference.

In fact, many things were working out much better for him since Mo's return. For instance, he regularly took him to football training, took time to hear him out whenever he had things on his mind (as any ten-year-old often does), and, nicely enough, regularly slipped him a few pound coins with which to buy what he liked. Yeah, Mo was cool — more of a friend than a father really.

Vinny didn't intend to sacrifice his wicked hairstyle just because of that stupid wedding, not without a fight anyway. And it was possible that Mo might just stand up for him once more...

"I will forever lift my eyes to Calvary... to see the cross..."

The shrill voice from the kitchen drew Vinny out of his reflections. That was another thing he couldn't take, these foolish songs the woman kept dishing out every minute. They were a painful reminder of many Sunday mornings spent against his will sitting among all those dressed-up, smiling and chanting people at the local Baptist church. To be fair, his mother had let him off quite a few times, as she didn't attend the services much herself, and his grandmother had had to content herself with Nicole to accompany her.

Of Vinny's list of most hated things, church had to be the top item. What the hell was that fat, sweaty preacher talking about? Vinny certainly had no idea, and wasn't interested enough to want to find out. He usually couldn't wait for all the chanting and singing to be done with, so he could return to the real life outside. To add insult to injury, there was always some old woman down there to pat his head with long, bony fingers and comment in a squeaky voice, "What a nice boy you have here, Sister Kline." Like he was some pet or something!

The worst thing was that, since the wedding plans had started, his mother now went along every Sunday morning. This was seriously bad news for Vinny.

He was wondering what new excuse he could try for the following morning when the call came.

"Vincent! Come here, darling."

Vincent! How many times had he told her not to call him that? Vinny sighed as he shuffled to the kitchen. He didn't like that name. "Vinny" sounded much better.

Hair tied up in a red scarf, her glasses peering over the dead chicken she was busy seasoning, the grandmother was singing to herself.

"Yes, Grandma?"

The old lady turned and smiled at him. She was tall, the lines on her light-brown face running like tiny rivulets. "You want something to eat?"

"No, thank you."

"You want a drink? I make you a nice cup of chocolate..."

"No. Thanks. I'm all right. What time's my mum coming back?"

Expertly, Grandma dipped her hand in the bowl in front of her and proceeded to rub the seasoning all over the chicken, inside and out.

19

Vinny could smell the aroma of the herbs and spices from where he was standing at the kitchen door.

"She'll be back soon. She's at the salon getting her hair done, and you know these things take time. Here, take one of them bananas."

More to please her than out of genuine hunger, Vinny went to take one of the fruit from the bowl on the table.

Back in the living room he absentmindedly watched a game show on the TV. He wondered what Nicole was doing right now. Mo had taken her along to help him choose his suit, but they had probably finished long ago, and would now be having a nice time.

The sound of the key in the door had him on his feet and in the corridor.

"Hi, baby! Everything all right?"

Vinny nodded to his mother, watching her as she took off her coat and hung it up.

"What d'you think? You like it?" she asked, switching from one side to the other in front of the tall mirror. Her long hair was permed and stacked high on her head like a beehive, blonde streaks running throughout.

"It's all right. What time we going home?"

"In a little while. I have things to do with Grandma."

"Can I go outside?"

"It's gonna rain. Why don't you watch some TV?"

"I've been watching it all afternoon. I'll come back in when the rain starts…"

"All right, then. But stay around the block, OK?"

"Yeah."

Vinny was out of the door in a flash.

"Oh, that's nice." Mrs Kline said as her daughter entered the kitchen.

"You like it? I had to wait over an hour to get seen to. It was packed in there!"

But for the age difference and the smoother skin, Julie was an almost exact replica of her mother. She was just as tall, and had once been slim, skinny even — as required by the modelling career she was pursuing at the time. To all the boys in the neighbourhood and beyond, Julie had been the dream they all prayed to own. Her fine, oriental features and honey-brown skin turned heads wherever she went, and she grew up knowing that these assets allowed her to get away with almost anything.

On a par with her natural beauty, Julie also had a very sharp brain, of which she made excellent use. Some people might say she had become a woman without scruples, yet the subtle way beautiful women exert control over their prey always mystifies the observer. Julie had simply made the most of her physical gifts.

For her mother, the pride she derived from people's compliments of her child made her

21

overlook any faults Julie might have had. She'd had great hopes for her youngest child and only daughter, dreams of success she almost saw come true when Julie won a couple of local beauty contests as a teenager and was offered a modelling contract. But a pregnancy at nineteen had put paid to Julie's rise to the top. She gained a daughter, Nicole, but lost the waistline she was so proud of, and by the time Vinny was born she had passed the ten-stone mark. After that, rich foods and lack of exercise helped to keep her on the plumpish side.

"Your aunt Peggy called. She says she'll come one week early to help."

"That's nice," Julie said, switching on the kettle.

"And Lucille's coming back from Guyana just in time for the wedding," her mother added.

Julie wouldn't have missed her cousin if she couldn't make it, but she was family, she supposed. For many reasons, Julie and Lucille had never quite got on. They were first cousins, born the same year, but had never been close.

"You know what, Mum? This friend of mine at the hairdresser was telling me I should have gone to Manchester to get my wedding dress. She got hers down there last year for a better price than it costs in London."

"It was probably not as nice," her mother commented.

"It was a really pretty dress; I was at her wedding…"

Mrs Kline washed her hands at the sink. "Well, yours is already ordered. And anyway, if you're gonna spend seven hundred pounds on a dress, fifty pounds more or less makes no difference… Oh, before I forget: your friend Sonia called for you. She wanted to know what she should buy you as a present."

Julie sat near the window, sipping her tea. "I don't even know what to tell her. I'll probably end up with a lot of things in double."

"That's always the problem when you invite so many people."

Julie looked at her mother. "You think we invited too many people?"

Mrs Kline shrugged and sat at the kitchen table. "No, not really. After all, it's better to have a big wedding than a small one."

"Oh, this one's gonna be big. You know you always have people who turn up just like that." Julie sighed. " I'll be glad when it's all over. There's so much to do, it's starting to do my head in."

"Three weeks from now, you'll be a married woman," her mother said, carefully peeling a tangerine. Then she added, "At least I can go to my rest in peace after that."

Julie looked at her, frowning. "I wish you'd stop talk like that, Mum."

"I know, but that was my only wish: to have my one daughter married, like a respectable woman."

"You don't have to be married to be respectable, Mum. This is 1996."

Mrs Kline swallowed a segment of tangerine. "All the same, if you have children and no husband, it doesn't look too good."

Julie smiled and shook her head. "You're always so worried about what people think. Remember that people don't always get on; children have often got nothing to do with it."

"Well, that is why a woman must keep her head on. If you'd listened to me at the time you wouldn't have disgraced yourself and ruined your career."

"Please don't start that again, Mum. I'm doing fine." Julie made a good living as the owner and manager of a beauty and hair salon she had opened a few years earlier in nearby Camden, but somehow it wasn't as glamourous as what her mother had wanted for her. Old dreams die hard. Julie started to say something more, but her mother hadn't finished.

"You could have become one of them supermodel. Like that black girl... what's her name again? Naomi Campbell."

"I don't think I would want to be like her..."

Mrs Kline finished her tangerine and sighed. "Anyway, this is the right thing to do. And the children's father owes you that much, I think."

Julie got up and washed her empty cup, placed it upside down on the drying rack. "Where's Dad?" she asked.

Mrs Kline smirked. "You ever see him at home on Saturday afternoon? Today is Dominoes day. Tomorrow is football. Dem dyam man is all the same..."

Julie quickly switched topic. She knew the only time her mother lost her clipped English tones and slipped into her Caribbean dialect was to pass derogatory remarks about her slippery husband.

"I've got to call the garage to see if they've finished fixing my car. It's costing me a fortune, you know!"

Mrs Kline picked up on that. "Then why don't you buy something smaller? It will save you money all round."

"I don't like small cars, Mum."

Although the car cost her money to run and especially to repair, Julie wouldn't have dreamt of driving anything smaller than her beloved new BMW. She still felt sore at the unfortunate Indian woman who had crashed into her the previous week.

The bell rang, and she went to open up for Vinny.

"I told you it was gonna rain!" Julie told her son.

He followed her inside the kitchen. "Is Mo back yet?"

25

"Let me call home and find out..."

Mrs Kline looked at her grandson. "Why don't you call him 'Daddy' like any decent boy? Julie, I don't know how you grow these children."

Vinny had always called Mo by his name. In fact it was probably the very first word he had uttered as a baby. Julie left her mother and went to use the phone in the living room. She listened to the ringing tone for a minute before hanging up; no one was at home. Julie went back to the kitchen.

26

The cab driver's banter was going right over Mo's head, but he kept on with the occasional "Hm" and "Right" as if he was taking in the conversation. He didn't mind the man talking to him; after all, he had lived as a near hermit for the last few months. Apart from Julie (and that was another matter), Mo's verbal contact with outsiders had been limited to an infrequent chat with the local newsagent, a football fanatic, and with Emmett, the only "old friend" he had seen since his return. Emmett was actually just a school acquaintance, but since they were now living on the same street, he and Mo had had the occasional conversation.

"So, you're out for a night on the town, then?" the chirpy middle-aged driver commented with a knowing look at Mo's white shirt and grey flannel jacket.

Mo smiled. His dinner date was strictly that as far as he was concerned, but he shrugged smugly to humour the driver. "I'm ready for whatever…"

27

The driver laughed, then, without missing a beat, switched mode and unleashed a few chosen epithets on the driver of a van who had cut him too sharply for his taste. The seven o'clock news summary on the radio told of terrorist bomb-threats on the London underground... Thirteen Nigerians applying for political asylum were to be deported...

That warranted a dry comment from the driver: "I mean, you gotta draw the line somewhere, ain'it? Otherwise anybody can just come in the country and settle down..."

He turned to glance at Mo, whose face showed no emotion either way.

"Now, you tell me..." the driver continued amiably, "suppose I was to fly out to, say, Nigeria for instance, and try to claim social security."

Mo smiled. "I'm not sure they got that over there."

"There you go!" the driver said, right hand outstretched through the window. He cut on to the left lane and into Southwark Park Road. "It's not that easy for us to do the same thing, right?"

He was looking at Mo like he really wanted to know his opinion.

"I believe it's all down to money," Mo said. "People would leave their country if they could make a living safely elsewhere..."

"I mean, don't get me wrong," the driver interrupted. "I think it's good for everybody to have people from other races in this country...

but if you just open up the doors, we're soon gonna be a hundred million in here!"

Mo nodded and grinned at him. "And we'll all have a suntan."

The driver seemed to consider that for a few seconds, then he smiled broadly and shook his head. "You said it!"

Then he went on: "D'you know what my wife said to me last week? She said..."

Mo's mind was already away again. Once again, he wondered if accepting the dinner invitation from Carmen had been such a good idea. Now more than ever he needed to focus on the important step he was about to take, and not to get distracted by or tempted in any way towards other women. Come on, go and have dinner, enjoy yourself. She's your friend after all! a little voice said in his head. Mo was starting to identify this voice he kept hearing lately as the whisper of temptation... Still, he was in control here. In a little over two weeks he would be a married man with responsibilities and a vow to live up to. For better or for worse... He already had the suit hanging in the wardrobe!

Mo cut into the driver's monologue:"How long've you been married?"

"Twenty-seven years," the man said, almost proudly.

Mo nodded. "Tell me, what's it like?"

The driver blew his horn in despair at the inconsiderate driving style of someone in front of

29

them. "Put it this way: it's kinda like if you go to prison..." he said. "You gotta do the time, right... but you have regular time and then you have hard time." Seeming satisfied with his metaphor, he looked at Mo. "I done easy time so far..." Then he let out a raucous nicotine-ridden laugh.

Mo smiled at him; it sounded like a fair comparison.

"Here we are. What number you looking for?"

"Sixty-nine," Mo answered.

He paid his fare and walked up to the front door of one of the maisonettes. In the next garden, a noisy game of fly-catch had two young girls and a boy leaping all over the faded lawn.

The door had opened even before Mo could stick his index finger on the bell. "Hi! So you came after all..." Carmen's teeth were all out in the smile.

"Here I am," Mo said under her scrutiny.

She admired his neat clothes while he noticed her sandals and interior African robe.

"I thought you'd be ready," he said.

"Oh, I'm ready. I waited for you to show up before getting dressed." Carmen stretched out her left hand and held his jacket lightly. "Come on in — don't be afraid."

He followed her inside, laughing. "I'm not afraid."

Mo thought the room looked really nice. The fat cushions spread on the carpet and the lines of tall potted plants made you want to stretch on the floor and crawl like a lizard in the brush. The darkwood shelves of the cabinet were lined with dozens of different sized publications.

"You've read all these books?"

"Most of them," Carmen said. "Except the big volumes at the top; they're gonna take me a few years."

She invited him to sit in her large, swinging bamboo chair and put the remote control unit in his hand. "I'll be ten minutes. This is a video a friend of mine mixed. I want to use it with the kids. Tell me what you think. Rewind it..." Then she left him there and disappeared upstairs.

Mo rewound the video and pressed "play". Antelopes leaped, cheetah cubs were romping, and a herd of giraffes clipped the tops of tall acacia trees to a background of the hauntingly beautiful male voices of a Zulu choir. For a few minutes Mo got caught in the magical images and sounds, and his heart filled with a tranquillity he hadn't felt in a long time. The following clip showed a ballet performed by graceful young Asian women, Thais as far as Mo could tell, twirling and tiptoeing to The Wailers' classic *Pass It On*. Curiously, it was so well synchronised you would have thought the dancers could actually hear the music.

Mo turned as Carmen appeared behind him and placed her hand on his shoulder.

"What do you think?" she asked.

Mo took in her black waistcoat, frilly shirt and long skirt, the tightly curled hair tied on top in a red bandanna, and nodded. "Not bad..."

Carmen narrowed her eyes the way she did, and playfully poked him in the neck. "I was talking about the video!"

"Oh... It's beautiful," Mo said seriously.

"I'm going to use it at the nursery. The children will love it!"

Mo got up. "So, where are we going?"

Carmen was switching off the TV and video. "You know the Beach Hut?"

The name rang a bell. "I heard the name on the radio... I think," Mo said.

"It's a cafe-restaurant they opened not long ago in Camberwell. Nice place, great food. You'll like it," Carmen assured him while she fixed his shirt collar.

She picked up her keys and bag. "Let's go. I made a reservation."

They left the house. The children playing outside waved at Carmen. She unlocked the doors of her Volkswagen Golf and they drove off.

Mo watched the young woman's energetic driving style. Another driver intending to come out of a parking spot too lively earned a blowing of the horn.

"Don't worry. I'm a careful driver but I always anticipate other people's mistakes and warn them, you see."

"I see." Mo smiled, relaxing in the passenger seat and watching the early-evening activity on those South London streets he hadn't seen for a while. He felt glad now that he had listened to his little voice. Carmen had this calming, peaceful effect on him and he didn't know why. He always felt as if he'd known her for years — indeed, it was three years since they'd met — and yet today was only the fourth time they'd seen each other.

He had toyed with the thought of calling her since his return, dismissing it from his mind several times in the name of the "commitment" he had made. In the end, he'd tried the nursery number she'd given him three years before and surprisingly, or logically, it was Carmen who had answered the phone. She almost screamed down the line, recognising his voice first time. Mo had no choice but to agree to her dinner invitation, feeling warm inside that someone should hold him so dear and be so excited at his return.

Carmen... five feet five, looking like one of those long-eyelashed pretty black dolls little girls play with. You could look at Carmen's oval face and know what she was thinking. Mo had never, in all his life, met anyone quite like her. It wasn't that she was loud or extrovert in any way, yet you could always expect that young black sister to speak her mind and let you know what she thought — if the occasion warranted it. She had that complex mix of openness with just the right awareness of social conventions and decency, so

33

that she was never quite out of order anywhere. But Carmen was never misunderstood. Mo remembered how much caught unawares he had been the first time they met.

After the robbery, Mo had decided to get out of the jewellery business altogether and return to his first love. He'd spoken to Baloo on the phone and re-opened the studio, and bookings hadn't taken long to come in. Though he'd tried to get Sam back in the recording booth, his brother had kept making promises but not showing up, already too far gone to pick up his career again. Mo had solid credentials as a sound engineer, and he had learnt the insides of the producing game from the best. He had worked with a band on their LP all through the winter months, and with the release of the record they had started a UK tour. Mo had been trying to get the best out of a poor PA on a cold night in an half-empty Birmingham venue. Busy as he had been monitoring the band, he hadn't noticed the short woman who stood to the left of the mixing desk the whole evening. When she'd stepped up to him at the break, Mo hadn't been ready for it.

"Hi, my name is Carmen. I've been watching you all evening and I want to ask a favour from you. I'm a poet, and I have something I'd like to try — tonight. I would like you to ask the band if I could do one of my poems at the end of the show. It will only take five minutes." The young woman with the glowing white teeth and the woollen hat smiled, and added, "If you do me this favour, I'll forever be your friend."

Mo didn't know what to say at first. He saw no problem in Carmen's request, but he knew the band might not agree to it. But the guys were cool and said they'd give "Mo's friend" a break. So Carmen was introduced at the end of the show, climbed on stage and, on the back of a well-known Sade song, delivered a string of thought-provoking, conscious lyrics which left the audience dumfounded. They had come for a good time on smooth grooves, and the sight of this short woman walking up and down the stage dropping cultural bombs on them shook them up. They loved it — and so did the band, who insisted Carmen should do her poem all over again.

Mo couldn't believe it. When it was all over, he told Carmen, "You was bad. Check me out — we should record that stuff."

Calmly, she replied, "This is the first time anyone has heard my lyrics. I just wanted to know how it sounded. But I'll give you a call. After all, you're my friend now."

And she had left, after thanking the band. Mo heard from her a week later. She called the studio, said she was finishing work that month and was moving to London after that. She came to the studio in the summer. They spent time discussing her material, he showed her how he mixed the tracks, and she seemed very keen on learning everything.

Carmen was very intuitive, and very talented. Speaking with her, Mo realised he had never met a woman so steeped in black culture and history, such a keen observer of human behaviour, who could draw on references from her readings to debate on almost any topic. Yet he never felt preached to or overwhelmed by the type of biased views a lot of so-called "feminist" educated black women usually pour on men. Carmen was a proud black woman all right, but her militancy was balanced and never dogmatic. Mo had liked her right away, and she, with typical frankness, had told him that he was very cute, but she was not sexually active for the time being, and that she would work with him and see where it would lead to. Work first of all, she'd said.

Mo had enjoyed that time with her. Since his final break-up with Julie almost three years before he hadn't met anyone interesting enough to be serious about. He and Carmen spent one entire, platonic, amazing, emotional night in Cambridge before he went to tour the States with the band. Then he returned and found his world had crashed...

"That's the place." Carmen pointed to a shop front, through which he could see people hanging around a bar, chatting and sipping drinks. Carmen parked and they walked in. A polite waitress led them past the bar and through to the restaurant beyond high wicker screens. The walls were adorned with picturesque Caribbean country scenes, so big that Mo felt as if he were actually seated beneath the giant painted willow tree.

"Nice, isn't it?" Carmen said across the table.

"Yeah, they done it good." Mo was scanning the room, taking in the faces of the diners. Only five other tables were occupied so far. The music oozed out of small square speakers at the top corners of the room.

They ordered their meals. The drinks came first — natural juices, since neither of them drank anything strong. When the food arrived, Carmen tucked into her meal with enthusiasm, explaining that she never put on weight. Mo told her she could afford to. She laughed and asked him if he found her too slim. He shrugged and said she was "all right". He had not felt hungry before he saw the brown stew fish which covered the whole plate.

On the way back from clearing another table, the waitress asked if everything was OK and they both nodded eagerly, avoiding speaking while munching.

"You look nice with the beard," Carmen told Mo between mouthfuls.

He smiled.

"You know, I want you to tell me everything that happened to you these last three years... but enjoy your meal first."

"I guess we have to talk," Mo conceded. He didn't tell her how good he felt being with her now, but he thought she probably knew and felt the same. Their eyes talked while they ate. This was the best Mo had felt since his return. Once his stomach was full and the fish bones lay bare on his plate, he wiped his mouth and sat back.

"That was excellent. I bet you come here often."

Carmen swallowed. "I've been here twice before... but this is my first time with a man," she slipped casually.

They squinted at each other, falling back easily into the little comic routine both had enjoyed before.

"So, you was telling me they made you manager at the nursery..."

"That's right." Carmen put down her fork. "I told you I was gong to take over."

She had said that to him, the last time they'd met, a week after she'd gotten the job as a worker.

"So, what about the lyrics?" he asked.

"I've been working very hard. I've got some bad stuff. You're back at the studio, yeah?"

"Well... not yet." Mo wasn't about to tell her the truth yet, that he was giving up on that to get a regular job. Right now, it didn't feel right.

Between the first row of tables and the screens a narrow corridor led to the restrooms. From where he sat, Mo could see the crowd outside the glass front. Somehow, though, he didn't see the tall man until he was standing over their table. Dressed in a checkered shirt, big in body, the man was fixing Mo with dark eyes. Carmen sat very still, wondering, and for a few seconds Mo too wondered. But the bushy, greying beard and shoulder-length dreadlocks didn't throw him off for long. He got up, stared at the new arrival for several long seconds, until the big man opened his arms.

"Welcome home, Slide."

Mo felt a little pinch in his stomach; he hadn't been called that in a long time. Then he got in close and hugged the man.

"Man... I'm so glad to see you, Baloo."

A few of the diners looked on curiously. Carmen could see the emotion in Mo's smile. The two men sat, observing each other silently at first, then Mo said, "I almost never recognised you. "

"You grow beard as well," Baloo remarked.

He had never been one to smile much, but Mo knew him better than most, and he could tell that Baloo was happy to see him now. For Mo it was the same, a lot of memories rushing up.

"When did you get out?"

"Couple months after you leave town."

Mo nodded. There was a lot he wanted to talk about with Baloo; years had passed since they'd

39

been face to face, years which had brought many changes, many painful happenings that had affected them both.

Baloo seemed stuck for words; he just kept staring at Mo. Carmen was quietly observing the two men.

"So, where you at now?"

"At the base, same way."

"You're back at work?"

Baloo nodded slowly. "I have one or two good singers. You must pass, check me." He paused before asking: "You have any plans?"

Right then Mo felt the old confusion surfacing, which had been simmering inside him throughout the last few weeks. He said feebly, "I'm just trying to settle down first, you know..." and wondered if Baloo had heard about his imminent wedding. He couldn't tell, yet there was something in the man's voice, he was sure of it.

"I want you to be careful, Slide. Come check me, we talk..."

Just then a skinny brown boy came up and whispered a few quick words in Baloo's ear. The big man nodded and the youth walked away.

"I don't know what is in your heart, my youth, and I never got to tell you..." Baloo got up from the chair, looked at Carmen for the first time, and paused. When he turned back to Mo, his voice was somewhat lower: "I really sorry about Sam. I want you to know that... He was the best, the very best."

Mo knew the man spoke from the heart. He had been like a father to both of them since their teenage days, and the feeling had never died.

Baloo seemed to think about all this for a moment, arms to his side, his eyes lost somewhere in the mural. Then he touched Mo's shoulder. "Check me."

"I will," Mo said.

He watched Baloo's powerful frame move away, then stop. The man stepped back to the table. Leaning slightly down for confidentiality, Baloo told Mo, "Listen, Slide, I have to let you know: Fizzy's brothers — them know you're back. Them want to talk to you, that's what I hear."

Mo looked the big man straight in the eye for a few seconds, but didn't answer.

"Look after yourself. Peace," Baloo said before walking away.

Mo watched him step outside and get inside a waiting car. Carmen didn't ask any questions. She could see something was stirring inside him. Once she had paid the bill, she touched his hand lightly.

"Come, Mo. Let's get some air."

41

• I N N U E N D O S •

"You deserve better than this, Moses," Aunt Alda declared gravely.

Even his mother called him "Mo", but not Aunt Alda. Oh no! She was very "biblical" like that.

The phone rang and Aunt Alda got up, letting Mo off the hook.

"... Morning, Sister Blossom. How you do...?"

In his chair, Mo gazed absentmindedly through the window at the shoppers coming in and out of the Tesco supermarket. Aunt Alda's house was the same as it had been twenty years before, when his mother used to leave Sam and him in her charge while she went to her evening job. Only the surrounding area had changed somewhat, but not that much. This part of Hackney had retained its village-like character, even with the tall tower blocks standing over Well Street.

Mo had dropped in on his aunt on his way back from dropping Vinny at his friend's home for the day. The day before, the little boy had

42

gotten in trouble with his mother about something to do with a fight in the local playground, and she'd decided that he wouldn't be allowed to spend the day with his friend as arranged the previous week.

Vinny's behaviour was a constant irritation to his mother. Twice he had had to change school due to fighting. Mo found it hard to blame him, though; he knew the little boy was short tempered, but he never actually started a fight. Vinny was quiet for a boy his age, almost brooding at times, and he liked to be left in peace. But woe upon whoever dared to come and distress him! Mo had seen him fight once or twice, and the boy was actually good at it. He could fight boys older and bigger than himself and still come out on top. Though Mo felt it good to know he could take care of himself, he knew Vinny would have to quell his temper to get through in life.

Still, Mo didn't think the punishment was deserved or fair, so he'd argued on behalf of Vinny. Sometimes he felt Julie was too hard on the boy. He'd told her so a few times, and that was when she would usually turn around and remark pointedly that she was the one who had coped with him all these years while he was away "having a good time". Julie's tongue could be like a viper at times. Everyone who knew her agreed on this; whether they would say it openly or not was another matter. The number of enemies she had made in the area since her schooldays was considerable, but she had four older brothers and this fact alone had saved her more than once from being properly dealt with for her impertinent ways. But on this occasion, she had simply shrugged and told Mo he was free to take Vinny to his friend's house himself.

Now Vinny was safe, and Mo felt heavy from the breakfast Aunt Alda had insisted on cooking for him. The downside of it was that the old lady had then proceeded to start on him about his planned wedding. She was his late father's younger sister, tall for a woman, lean and black like that side of the family all were. She deeply loved Mo, who she reckoned was the exact stamp of her father. Mo had never known him, as the old man had died in Jamaica before he was born, but the one black and white photo Aunt Alda had shown him sure made her point. Sam looked more like their mother, a little lighter in complexion and more stocky, but Mo belonged to the Aldridge family. From their East Indian great-grandmother he had inherited the dark tone of skin and finely chiselled nose and mouth, the tightly curled hair, the thin eyebrows and slender hands. Women always commented on his hands. Aunt Alda loved to repeat that her grandmother had been the prettiest woman in the whole of St Mary.

Another family trait of the Aldridges was the irrepressible tendency to tell it like it is. Aunt

Alda had taught Mo and Sam again and again that lying was the worst sin, stealing coming a close second. Though not overtly religious, the old woman had very clear concepts of right and wrong, and had done her best to drill them into her own two daughters and her brother's sons.

Aunt Alda put down the phone and Mo thought he would get her started on another topic. "When last you hear from Lucinda, Auntie?"

His cousin was the same age as him, and he hadn't seen her for six years since she had settled down in Jamaica and got married.

"She write me last month, you know. She's all right..." Then Aunt Alda showed that she wasn't that easy to fool. "I know you don't want to listen to my advice, but you is me nephew and I don't want you to make a mistake."

Mo sighed. He had come to ask her whether she would, after all, be attending the wedding, and he was getting more of an answer than he had expected.

"I know what I'm doing, Auntie. She's got my children; I might as well do the right thing."

Aunt Alda looked at him from behind her glasses. "There's a way which seemeth right unto a man..." she declared sanctimoniously.

"I know, I know, but I've thought about it. I have to settle down."

"But you don't love her!" Aunt Alda's gaze was that of a mother to the son she knows better

45

than he does himself. She shook her head slowly, seemed deep in reflection for a while. "Let me tell you something, son: you're just young and you don't know certain things. These people are very funny, you know, and you might not find out until it too late."

Mo had heard that from her before. He knew Aunt Alda was very "nationalist" like that. Not that she didn't have friends from various other Caribbean islands, and got on well with them, but she still had her own little reservations about certain things.

"Come on, this is England," Mo said. "We're all the same black people."

He saw Aunt Alda push out her mouth in a typical manner.

"Moses," she said, "I know you love the children, them and them need you too, but remember this: you and them is blood... you and the mother is not and will never be."

Mo had no answer to that unbeatable logic.

Aunt Alda sighed deeply. "Anyway, I done tell you how I feel. I stop talk now, else you start to hate me for it."

"Auntie, don't talk like that."

Mo stayed with Aunt Alda until after midday. Once outside, he walked slowly through the market, loitering in the sun, buying himself a couple of things he didn't really need just for the sake of buying. Walking on leisurely into Morning Lane, Mo reached Mare Street and made for a passing 38 bus. He couldn't quite tell why he hadn't bought himself a car. He had enough money for one, but he kept postponing it, taking buses and cabs without feeling any discomfort. Many years spent on the road had given him a taste for being driven. The same applied to the phone — not that there were many people who would have called him, but Julie for one had been on his case about that. Mo told himself he would take care of that next week.

The bus halted at Dalston Junction and a group of noisy teenage girls came on. They were probably no older than thirteen, but from their showy attitude and unrestrained conversation you would have thought they were three or four years older. In the opposite seat across the gangway, a visibly pregnant woman settled in with her shopping bag. Distracted by the thoughts shuffling in his mind, Mo didn't notice right away, but eventually felt the stare coming from her direction. He focused on the woman in the light blue dress. The sound of her voice reached him clear enough.

"Mo?"

It couldn't be, he thought. But it was. Bigger in all senses of the word, but Angie it was without a doubt.

Mo stepped to the other side, sat beside her.

"I knew it was you!" Angie squeezed his hand into her own, smiling broadly. "When did you get back?"

"About three months now. But you're looking good, Angie..."

The young woman raised her eyebrows comically. "Don't be funny, Mo. Look at the state of me!"

"No, serious. You're all nice and shiny."

Angie realised that, compared to the slim, drawn girl he had once known, she must be looking nice, pregnant or not. She laughed. "I'm shiny all right; it's the sweat from carrying all this shopping from Ridley!"

Mo enjoyed the joke. He felt good to see Angie — little Angie who'd been through so much with his wayward brother. She had been totally devoted to Sam, though he'd treated her indifferently at best and badly quite often. Mo loved Angie for her simplicity, her loyalty, and had done his best to help her whenever. Now she wanted to know what he had been doing, he asked about her life.

"I'm a married woman now, Mo... got married last year."

"Yeah? All right! Congratulations. Well, I'm a little late, I guess..."

Angie could see he was genuinely pleased for her.

"So what d'you want?" Mo asked, nodding towards her protruding stomach.

"I doesn't matter, as long as the baby's healthy." She shrugged, adding, "I was gonna ask when I had the scan but I think it spoils everything, you know what I mean?"

"You're right," he agreed. "Do I know the father?"

"I don't think so; he comes from outside London. He's a working man — BT."

Mo smiled. "I'm happy everything's turning out for you, Ange." He'd noticed she hadn't mentioned Sam, and he wasn't about to bring up that memory now. It wasn't necessary.

Angie asked: "So what're you doing now? Back in the music business?"

"Not yet," Mo said. "To tell you the truth, I'm following you. I'm getting married at the end of the month."

Angie opened wide eyes. "Really? And you just got back!" She watched Mo's face to check whether he was serious. He was. "Wicked, Mo!" She squeezed his hand again, then asked: "So, who's the lucky lady?"

Mo paused before answering, because he thought she would guess, and also because most of the people he knew seemed surprised at the news. As far as he knew Angie had never had any problems with Julie... But he saw her smile diminish a little.

"Not Julie...?" she said.

There it goes again, Mo caught himself thinking.

Angie looked outside. "I'm getting off at the next stop," she said. "I live just round the back of

these shops. You must come and see me soon."
She told him the name of a road and a number.

"When's the baby due?" Mo asked

"Not for another two months... I can't wait!"

Angie got up carefully, Mo steadying her
against the shaking of the bus, picking up her bag
for her.

"I'll pass and look for you before that, OK?"

"Any time, Mo. You'll always be welcome."
Angie gave him a little peck on the cheek before
getting off the bus. "Come and see me next week,
make sure!" she told him from the pavement.

Mo nodded and smiled to her, then watched
her wave him goodbye and walk away slowly, her
belly in front.

Mo got off soon after, walked up St Paul's
Road then cut left, taking his time. Willow Bridge
Road, where he was now living, was wide enough
for only two cars. Most of the houses had
garages, but on certain days, when residents
parked in front of their homes, like today, only
one vehicle could drive through at a time. Mo
watched two drivers gesticulate at each other
through their windscreens as to which one should
reverse and give way. The Burgundy BMW
parked in front of the gate told him that Julie was
home from the salon. Maybe for lunch, he
thought.

Monday morning. Twelve days to the wedding, according to the calender on the kitchen wall. (Mo realised he had actually been keeping count.) A bright and breezy Monday morning. Last night had seen one of these thunder storms which always seem to occur in summer when the weather gets too hot and the atmosphere becomes stifling.

Mo poured hot water from the kettle on to his herbal infusion bag in the mug, then unlocked the garden door and went to sit on the child's swing, feeling the gentle, early sun's warmth on his back.

Sipping the hot tea, he wondered once again if he should go to the job interview that afternoon. The letter the week before had taken him by surprise. Sure, he'd applied for the job as a "Housing Support Worker" with a Lambeth housing association, among several others, but with the state of the job market he hadn't been expecting much to happen. Mo had stumbled on the letter coming home one afternoon, and had thought it better to keep it quiet. There again, he caught himself, a big man, hiding things from his woman...! Julie regularly mentioned his job hunting — according to her it would be best for him to have a steady profession, since she was self-employed — but Mo hadn't really questioned the logic of it until today.

Swinging slowly he drank some of the tea, still undecided. From inside the house, sound waves reached him faintly from the CD playing on the living room system. Mo was all alone, and appreciated his solitude after a weekend which had proved restless enough. Julie had taken Nicole and Vinny with her when she left for work, to drop them off at her brother's house.

Mo put down his half-empty mug, stood up and stretched with a groan. Slowly, he loosened his muscles and joints, going through the warm-up pattern he knew so well. The tendons underneath his knees pained him as he tried to split, legs apart.

It was quite some time since Mo had stopped practising regularly. Though he still did workouts once in a while, he was no way as fit as he was when he had gone through three training sessions a week. As a youngster, Martial arts had provided him with an outlet for the surplus energy coursing through his body, and had taught him discipline and will-power, focus. Mo had never entirely lost those gains; the system he had been taught had moulded his character like clay in a potter's hand. Today he reflected, under the pain he could feel, that it was the start of his life as a young adult and his interaction with women that had slowly pulled him away from sports.

He breathed in and out deeply a few times, trying to empty his mind, the way he had learned studying meditation. But too many bits of information were creeping in there, like countless tiny worms, criss-crossing continuously, keeping his mind thinking, ticking over, never quite disconnecting.

He went to sit back on the swing.

He could feel hunger setting in. What should he have for breakfast? Or was it better to skip that and get organised for lunch, since it was nearing eleven o'clock...? He recalled Julie mentioning something about lunch and the freezer. That didn't appeal to Mo, whatever it was. Frozen food and microwave cookery were the mainstay with Julie and, despite having tried, for the sake of peace, not to pass any disparaging remarks about it, he just couldn't get into that. Although he had been born and raised in England, as far back as he could recall he and Sam had been brought up mainly on ground food. They would eat chips and spaghetti at school, just like their friends — but whether it was their mother cooking or Aunt Alda, proper Caribbean cuisine was the order of the day at home. Cornmeal or oats porridge, not Weetabix, were the staple breakfast diet. Even in Canada, where she was now living, Mo's mother would still have nothing to do with a microwave...

A little smirk appeared on Mo's face as he recalled the previous night. He reflected that, were it not for his seemingly strong and natural constitution, he would never be able to cope with Julie's "appetite" or the type of diet she was feeding him...

And this was another one of those little thoughts that were bothering Mo on this very pretty late-summer morning. In fact — no, this was a major cause for concern, and he was starting to wonder how many of the negative vibes he'd been feeling for the last few weeks stemmed from this... problem. If he had been in doubt about it until now, Mo could no longer refuse to face the truth: he was not sexually attracted to Julie any more.

The night before, Saturday night, Julie had insisted they go to an award ceremony attended by quite a few celebrities, among them champion boxer Lennox Lewis (whom Julia considered the "sexiest man on the planet"). But even he wasn't the prime reason: as one of a few companies sponsoring the event, Athena Hair & Beauty Salon, Julia's business, would get extra exposure, and Julia would certainly find a way to "represent" in person. Plus — and Mo was only dimly aware of this — her imminent wedding would be a sure hit with friends and a sore to her enemies, particularly those young women who had showered attention on Mo whenever he had been available throughout the years of their turbulent on-off relationship.

They'd gone down to the venue together, Julia dressed to kill. It was just as well Mo wasn't maintaining a low profile as such, because Julia received the amount of attention she wanted and more. But Mo had had a nice time, he had to admit. This being the first official function he'd attended since his return, he'd felt good being among his people again, part of the London scene in which he'd grown up. He met a few friends, who made him feel welcome, bought him drinks and asked him about his life these past years, and it all went well.

By the time they hit their bed (around the five-thirty mark) Mo was feeling good, content to slide into a soothing slumber. Julia... well, Julia was in a different mood altogether. The heights of her successful evening and the numerous cocktails she'd gone through had made her very lively indeed. Mo had been left no choice but to oblige her before finally crashing to sleep a few hours later.

As Mo had slept, Julia regarded his inert form. The physical contact between them since his return had been infrequent — maybe because Mo had changed, seemed more inclined to solitude and difficult to understand nowadays. Julia couldn't quite say what had happened, but Mo —

the Mo she had known so well, she thought —
had slipped away, and in his place now there was
a patient, mature and very quiet person. Sure
enough, the loss of his brother followed by an
exile of three years were bound to take their toll
on his personality, but Julia remembered a more
vibrant man, more extrovert maybe, with a
hunger of life that seemed to have vanished.
When she'd found out gradually that he wasn't as
responsive as before to her many charms, Julia
had watched him for a while, hadn't asked any
questions, just... watched him.

Right away, typically, she'd suspected he was
seeing someone else. Not that this would have
caused his lack of interest in her before... one
thing with Mo, he seemed to have been blessed
by Mother Nature with an inexhaustible strength,
and the one time he had had a relationship with
someone else, she hadn't been able to tell. No,
that wasn't it. It just seemed as though Mo didn't
have that hunger for her any more — she could
feel it — whereas Julia hadn't seemed to slow
down at all; she was as interested in sex now as
she had been at nineteen. In all their years
together, no matter how bad the fights they had
had, Julia had always used the craving Mo had
for her to bribe him to come back to her whenever
she pushed him too far and he left her. She'd
never worried: most of the things she'd done, and
hurt him with, she'd got away with because of
that sole fact. They just had that attraction for

each other, that animal instinct for each other's body, since the very first time...

Mo hadn't been Julia's first boyfriend. He knew she'd had a few experiences before meeting him and, although his enquiries had always been unwelcome, his own information had given him three names of local boys from the old schooldays. But of her own admission, her sex life had only really begun with Mo. She was the girl every boy in the district and beyond would have killed for: pretty, sexy, so attractive that she had few real female friends — or so it proved to be later, anyway. Mo, by contrast, was a quiet, mannered, almost shy boy. Never in the scramble for girls, he liked to watch and observe situations, only getting involved when necessary. He was a good student, and something of an electronics wizard. He was also the older brother of Julia's classmate, Sammy Aldridge, the boy with the voice that could, as their music teacher had told the whole class one day, "make angels cry". In any case, Mo hadn't looked for Julia; she'd come to the house with Sam one day to do some work, and they'd started talking. But it wasn't until about five years later, when Julia had started to get assignments as a model and Mo was working as a full-time engineer at Baloo's studio, that they'd met again at a local dance and it all started.

For years after that, some boys in the neighbourhood wouldn't talk to Mo. He even got into a couple of fights, against his will, caused by the intense jealousy he created by having Julia as a girlfriend. Quite a few times he endured nasty remarks about what a pretty girl like Julia was doing with somebody "black and ugly" like him. Mo wasn't ugly, he knew that. He was understandably proud of his dark complexion. Whether it was the contrast it provided that had attracted Julia or whatever else, she'd come to him. After that, it was like fire and lightning between them; sparks and flames that are never to be seen separately for too long. Sex between them had started as hot sex, then it had become crazy sex. If sex could kill they'd have been dead within six months. They say sex doesn't keep people together; it may be true, but Julia had caused Mo more problems than any sane man would endure from any woman, and he still came back every time.

So what was happening to him right now?

For him, the previous night's session had been unexpected and ultimately unwelcome. There's nothing quite as upsetting as sex when you're not in the mood for it, whatever the reason. In this case, it had left Mo a very bitter taste when he woke up. He couldn't say anything, but he knew that, if he was going to marry her, he and Julia were going to have to work out something like a rota — or rather, he would have to keep her to a level.

Mo believed that married life entailed certain changes in behaviour — rightly so — and as far as sex was concerned, he would deal with it, but not at the kind of rhythm he and Julia used to be on.

Well, that was what Mo had thought...

A few hours earlier, still in a semi-sleep, he had felt Julia throw one arm around him, and her warm body had closed the distance between them in the bed. Mo always slept on his right side, almost folded in on himself, like a baby in the womb. There was simply no other position he could fall asleep in. This unshakeable habit of his precluded any form of loving embrace that women might sometimes expect from their partners. So this very morning, when Mo had felt the insistent tugging at his body to turn around, he'd emerged from his sweet dreams to face a very eager Julia. He couldn't believe it! Only after he had performed once more, and slept again and woken up again, had the inescapable fact hit him: he was no longer sexually attracted to Julia.

And in twelve days' time he was going to take the big step with her!

This was going nowhere, Mo decided, and Monday was not the best day to tangle with vibes like that. He went back into the house and got busy playing music for a while. He'd bought a pile of CDs on Saturday, but had had no time yet to go through them.

The day before, Julia had reminded him that her mother expected them for dinner, and that she had done Mo's favourite: roast fish. The afternoon had gone fast. At the dinner table, it was mostly the two women doing all the talking. Julia's father had been quiet as usual; since everyone was used to that, no one had bothered him. Mo couldn't believe how calm and apparently serene the man was. Tall and bronzed of skin, Mr Kline never seemed in a bad mood — although it was hard to tell with him. Mo and he got on — as far as Mo could tell, anyway. In all these years, throughout the constant problems between him and Julia (about which her mother always had something to say), Mo had never heard her father speak ten words at any one time. A barber by trade, who had found employment as a railway worker on his arrival in Britain in the sixties, Mr Kline (or Sydney, as he was called by his wife) still cut heads for friends on weekends. Between this, his daytime job and the domino games at the local pub, Julia's father was rarely home. So when he was, he was a quiet, relaxing man. On that day, all those years ago, when a twenty-year-old Mo was arraigned before the Kline family for having made their daughter pregnant, Julia's father had said one thing and one thing only. When Julia's mother, who by contrast said plenty, had exhausted herself (she already suffered from high blood pressure at the time) with recriminations, directed mostly at Mo of course, the father had shrugged and said calmly: "No use getting mad; it's already happened."

And that was it. In all the subsequent conflicts over Nicole, when Mo and Julia, egged on by her mother, broke up, Mr Kline never showed Mo a bad face. Although Mo knew that the mother would always hate him inside for, as she put it so well, "destroying my child's career", the father was no problem.

Mo played a few tracks, started to record some on a cassette, then checked the time; it agreed with his stomach: time to eat! He went upstairs and showered, having picked his clothes for the interview. He would go out and eat, then take his time and make it to the appointment by three o'clock.

He had always dressed well, though not quite as flashily as Sam — but that was to do with their respective personalities. A blue shirt and thin black tie would do, with beige pants. He looked neat. A jacket? Well, maybe; he picked up one anyway. Julia had kept a few of the clothes he'd left behind and he still wore them sometimes, but on his return she had bought him a whole new set of suits and some casual wear from the States, where she visited her relatives each year.

The interview letter in his pocket, Mo left the house. A warm wind rustled the leaves around the edges of the wild laurel trees. Walking up the leafy street, Mo thought he was about ready to choose a car. He'd been seen by quite a few

61

people now, so he might as well get organised and pick up his life again. He wasn't going anywhere... Yes, he'd buy a car. After the wedding...

Mo decided he would walk up to the Latino restaurant near Pentonville Road; he had time to kill, and walking would help him relax. Crossing over the road to get to Upper Street, he noticed a car, the same dark blue Mercedes which had stopped to let him cross on the zebra crossing. It looked like... yes, it was following him. Mo frowned and glanced around, still walking. There wasn't much traffic, but the car was still crawling quietly a few yards behind him, so he stopped and waited, his head tingling with half-expectation.

The car was stopping by him. Mo very quickly took in three key elements: there were three men in the car, the driver was smiling at him, and only the man behind the sunglasses in the passenger seat was known to him. Mo instantly forgot about food. He stared and waited.

"Welcome home, Mo." The man took time dropping the shades from his eyes, looking straight into Mo's.

"Paolo," Mo said, nodding. He quickly glanced inside the back of the car but the man in there wasn't moving. He also wore sunglasses and a white baseball cap. From the driver's seat, the young-looking, frizzy-haired man in the open-neck shirt was still smiling at Mo. The medallion in shape of a bird's head that hung down his chest must have cost him a small fortune...

"I heard you was back in town, so I thought I might take a chance and visit you..." Paolo said with an engaging smile. "This is a nice area, Mo."

Unsure what to expect, Mo simply stood looking at Paolo with a bland expression. Their last encounter had been less friendly...

The driver was giving him the same snaky smile. Paolo shook his head. "I know what you're thinking, Mo, but don't be afraid. Me and you have to talk." He motioned towards the back seat. "Jump in, we'll drop you off where you're going."

Mo was thinking fast. It was three years later, but Paolo was still the man who had publicly promised to kill him. Things like that tend to stick in the mind, especially if the said person is known always to honour that particular kind of promise...

Mo said tersely, "Look, man — thanks, but I have an important appointment. I'll meet you to talk some other time."

Paolo's squint had nothing to do with the glare of the early afternoon sun. He still sounded almost kind, with just a little edge that gave away the meaning of his words. "You got an important appointment with me, Mo. Some bad things happened back then... I think we should clear the air between us."

Mo knew he was right. It had to be done.

"Don't be afraid," Paolo added, knowing that was one thing Mo had to react to.

The man with the white cap opened the back door, and Mo slipped on to the comfortable leather seat. They moved off. Mo eased back and waited, listening to the up-tempo music pumping at low volume. With his jacket and tie on, he felt overdressed. His abductors all wore summer shirts.

Without turning, Paolo said, "Mo, you know my little brother Raymond?"

So that's who the driver with the wild grin was! Mo remembered him as an unruly schoolkid, but that was it.

"He's just back in the country. Raymond..."

Raymond's strangely crazed grin reached Mo from the rear-view mirror. "Hi, Mo. Nice clothes..." The voice suited the manic look.

Raymond looked in his early twenties, Paolo was Mo's age; he knew that because they had done a year in the same class in third grade. He looked fat nowadays, the good life, no doubt... The car seemed to be heading towards Holloway, Raymond driving along as fast as the early afternoon traffic permitted. He took a sharp right, then cut through to catch the Hornsey Road, and entered a parking area behind a set of low blocks. Raymond manoeuvred the big car into one of the empty bays, switched off the engine.

Paolo sighed and turned to Mo. "Look, Mo. Let me first tell you I'm sorry about the last time...

OK? My brother was dead, and I thought you was involved... You can understand that?"

But for the intervention of a local ranking who happened to be on the scene that day, Paolo would without a doubt have fired the automatic he'd been pointing at Mo.

Mo looked at him. "I understand... I came back from tour and your brother was dead, and mine too. I didn't know anything." Out of courtesy, and because the situation was delicate just now, he added, "I'm sorry about Fitzroy, man."

Paolo nodded. "May God have mercy on his soul."

Mo watched, rather astonished, as Paolo signed himself. Raymond in the driver's seat did the same.

"What's done is done. They're gone, but we're alive — that's the way it turned out, right?" Paolo paused.

Raymond was busy watching the street through the windscreen. The young man next to him on the back might as well have been deaf and dumb. He didn't seem interested. Mo had a bad feeling in his stomach. Not fear, though — no, it was the expectation that he was going to hear unpleasant things, things he had run halfway across the world not to have to think about any more. But the memories were constantly being called back, it seemed. Because the reminding was coming from such a person as Paolo Sousay, Mo felt, well... apprehensive, to say the least. He

65

didn't know what it was yet, but something Paolo had to tell him would upset his spirit, Mo was sure of it.

"Like I said, I know you wasn't involved. I have nothing against you. Your brother killed mine, and that was his crime. I can't make you pay for it... Anyway, he's dead too."

Mo couldn't see the sun any more; he couldn't even see the man whose words tortured his wounded soul.

"Life must go on, Mo. So I'm not gonna waste my time and yours..." Paolo fixed him with penetrating eyes. With his neatly trimmed moustache and black curly hair, he could have been an actor, a leading man even. But he was Paolo Sousay, currently one of the biggest names on the London scene for "substances", successor to his deceased brother Fitzroy's clandestine fiefdom. And this was no motion picture!

"That day, the day the robbery took place..." Paolo stated slowly, "was a collection day. Your brother knew that. Someone set him up..."

Mo didn't answer, because he knew nothing either way. The tie felt tight around his neck.

Paolo's eyes seemed to get narrower as he continued: "Your brother had nothing on him when he died, and the police didn't find any money in his flat. He couldn't have spent thirty-five grand in one night..."

Paolo's words were sinking in Mo's mind. It was coming back now...

"What do you think, Mo?"

Mo looked at Paolo, incredulous. "Why d'you ask me? I wasn't even in the country, you know that!" he said.

"I know that... but someone must know," Paolo insisted. Then he added as an afterthought, "Unless he buried the money in a hole somewhere and died without telling anybody..."

Mo's jaws were tense. He looked through the window. If he could only wake up and find he had dreamed it all! For a long time after Sam's death, he'd often been woken up in the night by dreams in which his brother was still alive, only to face the crude reality of his absence.

He heard Paolo say, "You're gonna have to make good for the money, Mo."

"What?" It came out despite himself.

Paolo didn't look like he was joking. "You know we work as a family, right? When your brother robbed Fitzroy, he took money that belonged to all of us, to the family. We have to get it back. You understand?"

Mo understood all right, but certainly didn't see it like that. "Paolo, what are you saying? It had nothing to do with me. If I had been here it wouldn't have happened..."

Paolo sighed. "Maybe, maybe not... but this is where we are now. You're the next of kin; you inherit the debt." He paused, adding with a note of kindness, "It's nothing personal. I've always known you as a straight-up man. That's why I didn't send anyone. I come to tell you personally."

Mo's mind was spinning now; he couldn't even think straight.

"I'm not gonna ask you for all of it at one time, Mo," Paolo said, "but I'm gonna start sending for collection sometime soon... soon after your wedding."

Now Raymond turned to look at Mo, grinning as his brother said pleasantly enough: "After the honeymoon."

A fresh coat of paint had done away with the scrawled signatures and words of wisdom of the dozens of artists who had recorded at the studio over the years. It had become an essential part of the place's mystique, perpetuating the myth that the studio propelled youngsters into stardom, that every recording artist should write a few words, dated and signed, on the walls of the Aquarium. Due to its fame as a cornerstone of the reggae world in the UK, the studio was an essential stopping point for all visiting Jamaican musicians. They, and their crews of ghetto celebrities, also "signed the wall". Over the course of sixteen years, all kind of fishes had swum through that aquarium, and a lot of ink had covered its walls. When Mo had asked Baloo on arrival why he had wiped out this testimony of reggae music's history, the big man had simply shrugged and said, "Different time, different vibe."

Baloo was finishing putting some horns on a track. Mo watched him work, as keenly as he had that first day he had entered the studio as a fourteen-year-old aspiring engineer. A couple of years later, when Sam had proudly announced one night at the dinner table that he was going to have a song released, both Mo and their mother had sighed it off, believing it to be another one of his usual tall tales. But the following weekend, Mo had come back from the studio astonished to have heard Sam's song being talked about as "wicked" by the famous producer Baloo. Even more incredible had been the apparently genuine offer from the same man to teach Mo the technicalities of music recording. It was like a dream come true. And then Sam's first single had made it to number one and stayed there for five weeks over the summer.

Though Mo had pursued his ambition and graduated from college, it was in this studio that he had learned the ins and outs of his trade. Not only that: in this very room he had learned from Baloo what it meant to be a man.

"Nice track," Mo commented as Baloo finally switched off and leaned back in the swivel chair. "Who's gonna voice it?"

"Some girl from South London — she sounds good."

Over the years, Baloo had worked with many up-and-coming singers and DJs, nurturing their talents, bringing quite a few to fame and fortune. He was a very knowledgeable man when it came to all types of music, although reggae was his speciality and great love. Augustus Ballantyne, nicknamed after the Jungle Book character, had started back in Jamaica in the footsteps of his uncle, one of the legendary producers of the sixties. Baloo was a living encyclopedia of reggae music, able to quote the title, the year of release and the label of any song at an instant's notice. He usually worked at the mixing desk from early afternoon right through until the early morning hours, breaking only for food and ganja — and even that was taken care of on the spot. Mo had spent years working with him, as an apprentice at first, then as a fully-fledged engineer, and had earned himself credits for his production skills.

Beyond music, from Baloo he had absorbed knowledge which proved invaluable in his life as an adult. Literally living at the Aquarium around the clock, Mo had become mature under the big man's guidance and advice. The position had also given him status in the community.

Five feet eleven and weighing seventeen stone, Baloo was known as a calm, placid man who never raised his voice. Even in the tough world of reggae music he had no known enemies — or at least no one had ever been foolish enough to come up against him. But he didn't suffer fools gladly. The fateful events of that November night several years back had proven how dangerous it was to provoke Baloo's wrath.

They talked of this and that. Baloo built himself a good spliff while Mo told him briefly of his travels. The big man looked up when Mo told him he had passed through Jamaica, apparently only a few months before Baloo himself went there. After his release, he'd gone to the countryside for six months to meditate and rebuild himself mentally. There he'd embraced the Rastafari faith, healing his tormented soul. Mo and Baloo reasoned for a while, never touching on the past — but they both knew it couldn't be avoided for long.

"Paolo came to look for me," Mo said finally.

Through puffs of aromatic smoke, Baloo's eyes focused on his friend. He waited.

"He said I have to repay the money Sam took from Fitzroy..."

Baloo took another draw, exhaling powerfully before asking, "How much?"

"Thirty-five g's."

Baloo said nothing, so Mo asked: "Is he lying?"

Scratching the back of his head, the big man told him, "Sammy hit him on a collection day... He knew what he was doing."

Once again, that innuendo... Mo shook his head gravely. "The police didn't say anything about any money; they didn't know about it. Unless they took it for themselves..." Mo had spent all night running through his mind every bit of information he knew about his brother's death. As always, he'd had to sort out the rumours from the actual facts.

72

"Maybe him hide it somewhere safe," Baloo suggested.

"I didn't find anything at his place; the police searched Angie's flat..."

Baloo seemed sombre. He muttered, "He could have put the money anywhere. The way him was hooked dem time deh, him wasn't thinking straight."

"You're right," Mo agreed, still feeling bad having to say that about his own brother. "He had to be fucked up to go and rob a bad man like Fitzroy!"

A thought hit him, and he asked, "What about Lucky? Maybe Sam gave him the money to keep..."

Baloo's face broke into a rare sneer. "I buck up Lucky couple months after I come out; him never have two cents to rub together."

Lucky was another one of those names from the past Baloo didn't want to hear too much about. He had been Sam's partner in and outside the studio. A promising young DJ that Baloo had groomed for success, Lucky had sunk into drug abuse at about the same time as Sam. Who had corrupted whom? No one knew.

"What you think I should do, Baloo?"

There was no easy answer to that, they both knew it. What they also knew was that Paolo Sousay was a very serious man when it came to money. He was one of five sons of a Trinidadian family who'd more or less monopolised the traffic of narcotics in East London. His oldest brother was serving two life sentences for murder, the next one had escaped to the Caribbean a few years earlier after a drug bust. Fitzroy had been a drug don and a pimp until his death at the hand of Sam three years earlier. Paolo was left to take over the family business. He proved to be the most cunning of them, operating with caution through middlemen he controlled with a iron hand. He was also, or so the rumours had it, protected by certain local police officers to whom he made regular generous "donations". Stories of Paolo Sousay's ruthlessness in dealing with cheats and debtors were common knowledge in the ghetto. In fact, a propensity to violence seemed to be an inherited genetic trait in the family...

"Really and truly, you don't have nothing to do with this business, Mo."

That didn't exactly answer Mo's question. "What's gonna happen if I refuse to pay?" he asked

Baloo thought about this before replying. "The guy know you're my boy, still... but with him, you can't take no chance. Him crazy enough to try and hit you..."

Mo kept quiet for a moment, thinking it over. There seemed to be no way out. Even if he had the money, in principle it was wrong to hold him responsible. "I better get myself some protection then..." he said.

Baloo relit his spliff, then looked deeply into Mo's eyes. "You know I can't get involved in no rough stuff; they'd send me back down fast... Still, I can't stand aside and let you get hurt, you know that."

This was obviously a serious dilemma for him. Sighing, he continued: "I should never have asked you to make the move for me."

Mo could hear genuine sadness in Baloo's voice. He had always known the man felt responsible for everything that had happened. But Mo also blamed himself. If he had used the contacts Baloo had given him and got rid of the stuff instead of giving in to Sam's insistent pleas, maybe nothing would have happened. Yet maybe Sam would still have slipped and turned rotten all the same...

Then again, thinking like that, Yappy was the cause of all this nightmarish saga.

At the time, Yappy had been Baloo's friend and partner. Together they'd opened the studio back in the mid-seventies. Baloo took care of the musical side of things while Yappy, more outgoing and extrovert, acted as a manager and accountant. It all went well until, eventually, Yappy, like so many before and after him, got involved with drugs and quickly became a secret abuser. Secret he had to be, because he knew fully well that Baloo was totally against narcotics and even refused to work with any artists he knew to be drug-takers. But Yappy had gone even further.

In his role as manager he had easy access to the business funds, and so one day he'd decided he would "borrow" some money and make a buy. Once he'd turned it over, he told himself, he would put back what he had taken out and make a nice little profit in the action. Unfortunately, through rumours, Baloo had found out about the scheme and confronted Yappy, who had had the audacity to hide his stash on the premises. Hooked as he was by that time, Yappy had the nerve to want to fight Baloo to get his stuff back. In the confrontation that followed, Yappy got badly beaten up and hit his head against the corner of a metal cupboard. He died in hospital. Baloo was arrested, tried and sentenced to twelve years. He'd served seven before making parole. Baloo had managed to hide the stash of drugs before the police arrived, so when Mo went to visit him, he'd asked him to retrieve it and give it to some guy he knew, who would deal with it and so get back the money Yappy had taken. Mo's mistake had been to mention this to Sam...

Baloo was pulling long and hard on his spliff, observing Mo through the smoke. The studio was quiet now. Mo knew Baloo well enough to feel there was something he wanted to say, but he waited while the smoke filled the mixing room, drifting over the desk in little lazy clouds.

Finally Baloo spoke. "I don't know if I should tell you this, because it's only rumours I heard at the time..."

"Tell me what?" Mo asked, squinting intently at his mentor.

Baloo took his time before coming out with it. "Maybe Sammy heard it from somebody, maybe that is why him do it..."

Mo was curious now. "What you talking about, Baloo?"

A little pause again. Baloo was not a man to spread rumours. "You know, when you're inside you know more about what's happening on the street than if you was there..." He looked straight at Mo. "Some people say it was Fitzroy's people them who robbed your jewellery store."

The information travelled sluggishly inside Mo's overtaxed brain, finding its way along the chain of hypotheses about the whole drama. It sounded very tempting to accept the idea; if it was true, Sam's apparently crazy move wasn't so crazy after all.

"Like I said, it's only a rumour. There's many guys out there who could have robbed your business... But it's possible."

The perpetrators of the jewellery store robbery had never been caught. After much haggling with the insurance company, who suspected a criminal scheme, they had paid for the loss. But by then Mo had decided not to reopen the store anyway.

Mo said, "If it's true, I don't owe them anything. Fitzroy took from me, Sam took back from him."

But was it true? Mo was wondering who could verify this crucial piece of information. Not Paolo, surely...

Baloo would say nothing further about it. This was just like him: never say anything you're not sure of. He always spoke sparingly, especially with strangers, and never about people's business. But this was Mo...

The big man looked straight at his friend. "Fitzroy used to stick up and things before he started running drugs..."

"I have to find out for sure."

Both of them sat silent for a while, Baloo running a tape for the session. His mind adrift above the musical waves, for a brief moment Mo could almost feel Sam's presence in the little room, leaning against the master tapes' metal cabinet as he used to do. Then a couple of musicians Mo didn't know arrived and Baloo started to talk business with them. Mo hung around a while, then took his leave.

Baloo walked him to the upstairs door. "Maybe you have other things in mind, but you can do some work down here if you want, you know. I 'ave some tracks you could check out for me..."

Mo shrugged. "I might just do that, Baloo. Soon..." It would be so nice to forget everything and lose himself in music once again; it was so true that "when it hits, you feel no pain"... Mo thought of something. "You gonna come to the wedding?" It almost felt like talking about someone else's.

Baloo made an undecided face. "I don't too go out more time, you know." He put his hand on Mo's shoulder. "Still, I will try and pass..."

"All right. Bring Denise along," Mo said.

Baloo made another face. For some reason he didn't seem sold on the idea. He looked Mo in the eyes. "Don't do anything unless you check me, all right?"

He knew Mo was not impulsive, but Baloo could see how the events linked to Sam's death were affecting his friend. He knew Mo had to work things out for himself and find peace inside. He also knew a way to get Paolo off his back...

Mo stretched fully on the low sofa, absorbing himself totally for a few minutes in the thick black Japanese characters on the printed fabric, as a way to empty his mind. The turbulence of his thoughts made him feel tired — or at least he felt he could easily sink into a forgetful sleep.

Through the hatch that opened to the adjoining kitchen, Carmen's illuminating semi-smile appeared. "What would you like?"

Mo shrugged. "What you got?"

Carmen always seemed to have the most exotic flavours when it came to tea. Being a committed vegetarian, she was also an expert cook, as far as Mo had found out, and generally researched anything to do with nutrition and herbal medicine. He recalled now that tea was one of her areas of expertise.

"Well, you can have peach, lemon grass, verveine... or apple and cinnamon..."

Mo smiled despite his gloomy thoughts. "I think I'll go crazy and have a cocktail... say apple and cinnamon and verveine."

"Great idea." Carmen nodded before disappearing.

Mo closed his eyes against the setting sun that streamed through the open curtains. On leaving Baloo he had wandered out of his old area, absorbed, and walked all the way to Newington Green. He didn't really know where he was going, just that he was in need of time to himself, to work out a solution to his crisis. He had returned to start over, having buried the past, but now the past, which had been slowly creeping up on him over the last few weeks, had suddenly stepped right up to him.

So turning a new page wasn't working too well! This afternoon, while walking along like a lost soul, he had wondered for the first time whether coming back had been such a good idea. But he had quickly banished the doubt from his mind, telling himself he was going to sort it all out, straighten things up.

The first thing he'd resolved was that he didn't feel like going home. It was much too early, Julia would be at work until eight or so, and Nicole and Vinny were at their cousins' house. Naturally enough, because there really was no one else he could have gone to the way he felt, Mo had called

Carmen's workplace... and, naturally enough, she'd asked him first why he had not called her all this time. It had been, what, five days since their restaurant date, Mo had calculated after leaving the phone booth. He recalled having promised, after she'd given him a playful little kiss on the lips when he'd walked her to her front door, that he would call her by the weekend.

But then so many things were happening around him, that the days went by without him even noticing.

He was now ten days away from his own wedding, and he couldn't feel it. Mo had always imagined that a man about to take that major step in life must surely *feel* something, whether it be impatience, joy, anxiety, fear even... But not him. He couldn't feel anything, not so far at least!

As the bus taking him to meet Carmen had passed over Tower Bridge, the sun's rays on the river called up images of beauty and calm on a beach by the Indian Ocean. Flashes of those happy times flooded his consciousness for a brief instant, like clips from an MTV video.

South London was busy and bright as Mo had walked the last part of the journey to Carmen's house, brothas and sistas out in full force, sporting with graceful insolence the styles which trendy middle class fashion designers would launch as their own creations in next year's summer collection.

Carmen served the tea, and it was delicious and sweet. She looked happy to see him. Since, on first seeing his face, she had insisted that, whatever it was, he should not talk about it just yet, Mo took the time now to tell her the facts. He told her straight, everything he had found out, unloading his feelings about the situation, and she listened. Carmen could listen to him, he had noticed that on getting to know her at first. Mo talked and she would take it all in, asking the right questions when they needed to be asked — because that's all that someone needs sometimes. Mo sipped his tea, leaning back in the comfortable sofa, and looked at Carmen. Her thin plaits danced freely about her head, she wore track suit pants and a printed T-shirt with Malcolm X's face and the quotation: "To educate the woman is to educate the nation".

"If I had been here, it wouldn't have happened..." Mo said finally. Over the three years since that day, he had convinced himself that he could have prevented Sam from taking that desperate action.

"You can't be sure, Mo; your brother might have done it anyway."

"I could have talked him out of it, told him it wasn't a smart move, he wasn't thinking straight."

"You really think it's drugs that made him do it?" Carmen asked.

82

Mo didn't like talking about Sam's habit, as it had become. He didn't know how bad his brother was on it until too late. "That shit makes people think they're invincible. He wouldn't have done it sober."

"Maybe you're right," Carmen said. Then she added, "But remember, at first you thought he'd done it for money or drugs; now you've found out he did it out of revenge..."

Carmen was right; it wasn't as it had originally seemed.

Things were still bugging Mo though, little questions he couldn't answer. How did Sam find out about Fitzroy's involvement? Was that even true anyway? And who had tipped Sam on robbing Fitzroy, since everybody seemed to think he had inside information. Mo couldn't help feeling there was more to the story.

"I went away to forget, and I couldn't," he told Carmen dejectedly. "I came back to put the memories to rest, but they won't."

After a little pause between them, Carmen said, "They say when a person dies unjustly, his ghost stays around and haunts the living until justice has been done."

"Who's 'they'?" Mo asked, doubtful.

"All right — my mother says..."

They both laughed. Thinking about it, there might be some truth in that saying, Mo agreed. In any case, the spirit of Sam wasn't at peace.

"You and Sam were close, right?" Carmen asked.

"He was my only brother, I got nobody else." It felt almost painful to say that, and Carmen must have sensed it.

She said, "He went away while you weren't there. He must be trying to tell you something."

Mo looked at her strangely. He didn't want to get too deep into some mystical trip, yet he had experienced things in his life which made him reluctant to dismiss the reality of such concepts.

They said nothing for a while. Carmen poured out some more tea, went to change the Tracy Chapman CD in the stereo. "Play it again," Mo said. And she did. The sun was getting lower and Mo didn't feel like talking much, wanting merely to escape the depressing thoughts in his head, if only till tomorrow. Carmen brought out some scented oil, an African formula, she said, and slowly massaged Mo's temple and head, soothing him, more like a mother than a lover, though she was neither.

Mo fell asleep, he wasn't sure exactly at what point.

He woke up to semi-darkness and the aroma of cooked food.

It was after nine when Carmen finally drove him up to Elephant and Castle station.

The stone had lost some of its whiteness and a couple of bird droppings specked its top edge, yet the rectangular area it marked was free of weeds. Mo closed his eyes and communed for an instant with the spirit of his brother, while Nicole, by his side, made a silent prayer. There were few visitors to the cemetery on such an early morning, Saturday being commonly devoted to more worldly activities such as shopping or washing the car. It had occurred to Mo that people tended to visit the graves of their dear departed more in the winter; somehow this seemed to be the season most appropriate to that particular melancholic atmosphere that floats through burial grounds. All the same, death itself has no favoured time of the year, as everyone knows...

Mo had gotten up early to come and pay his respects, not only because the coming Tuesday would mark the third anniversary of Sam's death, but also because he had not yet been there since his return. Maybe subconsciously he still thought of what Carmen had said. The past three days he had spent in quiet contemplation of the loss he felt inside him, and now more than ever he needed to be here, even if it was but a gesture, because a piece of his heart was lying there also, underneath the sun-warmed stone.

Nicole had volunteered to come along, and Mo felt good about that. Sam had adored his niece, and she in return had grown up with a special bond for her Uncle Sammy. Even at the worst points of her parents' stormy relationship, like the time when her mother took a police injunction to stop Mo from seeing the children, Uncle Sammy had still managed to build bridges for Nicole's sake. Nicole and her uncle were an item, but Mo remembered that she had not shed a tear at the funeral. The loss had been sudden and brutal for a nine-year-old girl, but Nicole did all her crying in private. Today she had swapped her beloved jeans and T-shirt for a simple white linen dress, and stood now calmly before Uncle Sammy's last resting place.

"Have you been here since?" Mo asked his daughter.

She surprised him. "I came with Aunt Alda to bring flowers to Grandad last year."

Aunt Alda made regular visits to her brother's grave on the other side of the cemetery, and it was she who also kept Sam's plot weeded.

Nicole looked up at her father. "Dad, do you think Uncle Sammy is in heaven or in hell?"

Drifting as he was on memories, Mo hadn't expected the question. He asked, "What do you think?"

Nicole said tentatively, "Grandma said people who don't go to church to repent their sins go to hell when they die."

Mo sighed. He had had a hard time with Nicole's mother, but the pseudo-religious dogma the woman tried to push on to her granddaughter was another sore point altogether. Gently, he put his hand on Nicole's shoulder. "And how would she know that?"

Nicole shrugged. "That's what they say at her church..."

Mo asked her again, "And that church parson... or preacher... who taught her that; how does he know that?"

Nicole raised her finely arched eyebrows, the way she did when asked something she didn't know.

Mo said to her, "He's never died and come back; he doesn't know."

He realised then that he'd never had a chance to discuss this kind of thing with Nicole, now that she had become almost a teenager. He could see her grandmother's doctrines hadn't penetrated too deep into the twelve-year-old's consciousness — so far. Calmly, Mo explained to her what he knew for sure. "We all have to die some day, and none of us knows what happens after. All the people who tell you this and that, because they read it in a book written by other people... they don't know. You see, everybody has the right to believe in whatever they want..." He stopped and thought about the irony of it before continuing. "You used to believe in Santa Claus, right? That some old white guy with a white beard and a red suit was bringing you presents?"

Nicole put on her disdainful look, and Mo laughed.

"All right, you see what I mean. Now, why do parents tell lies like that to their children?"

"That's only for little kids, though!" Nicole pointed out.

Mo nodded. "Right, but you know something? Adults are just like little kids. They need to believe in things they don't see; they need to dream too. Life here is sometimes too hard otherwise." Mo stopped and checked himself. A thought had just come up that he couldn't remember ever *knowing* as such. "Adults need to believe they have a father, a 'dad' who's gonna pat us on the head and say 'well done' when we do good and who gets angry when we do bad. That's what all this church religion is about really."

Nicole smiled at the comparison. Mo wondered how far he could discuss these topics with his daughter — but then, she was not a young child any more, he realised. Nicole was a twelve-year-old who thought like a sixteen-year-old. That was the way they grew up in the nineties!

She asked, "So, all these people talking about heaven and hell...?" This point seemed to puzzle her; why invent things like that?

Mo shook his head. "Heaven is here on earth, and hell as well... It's the things you go through and the happiness or the suffering you feel inside."

Nicole listened. You could see the concentration on her youthful features.

Mo smiled at his daughter. Missing her had brought out more love for her from within himself. "Look, Miss..." He called her "Miss" quite often, though not consciously. "The only thing that matters, the only thing you can do here, is try and do your best, try to love people, to respect people... That means you've got to love and respect yourself first, right?"

"Yes."

"You love God and pray to Him, but don't try to imagine Him. Our minds are too small for that."

Nicole understood what he told her, Mo knew that.

She asked, "So where do you think Uncle Sammy is?"

Mo brushed back her silky hair. "He's gone... but because of the things he did for you, he will always be in your heart."

Nicole's eyes strayed towards the white headstone for a second. She sighed, but not sorrowfully, nodded, and asked, "We gonna go see Grandad's grave?"

"Come on... You remember where it is?"

Nicole took her father's hand, led him along the rows of graves to the far left side of the cemetery.

When they got home, Vinny was practising his kicks on the front lawn, bouncing the ball off the low boundary wall. Mo played with him for a couple of minutes, gave him a few pointers. He'd been a good player as a boy, though Sam had had more talent than him and could have made a top-league team if he'd taken it seriously.

Vinny stopped short of taking a shot. "Oh yeah — Uncle Baloo called for you..."

Uncle Baloo. That was the right name for the man, Mo thought to himself. Baloo loved the children as his own. "What did he say?"

"Uh... he said to call him," Vinny answered, unsure if there was more of a message than that.

Mo got Vinny to do a couple of headers, showing him how to hit the ball full on the forehead, then went inside. Julia zoomed past him in her dressing gown.

"I'm late... Everything all right?" She was already up the stairs. "Where you going tonight?"

Mo wasn't going anywhere as far as he knew. He climbed the stairs. Julia was putting on her make-up in front of the bedroom mirror.

"I got no plans," he said.

She caught his eyes in the mirror. "You're not having a stag night?"

Stag night! That thought had not even entered Mo's head. He recalled Julia mentioning her "hen night" on Saturday night... tonight. He shrugged. "I'm not into that kind of thing..."

Julia stopped applying some mascara and turned to look at him. "What's the matter with you? Why you looking like that?"

"Nothing... I'm all right."

"You shouldn't go to the cemetery if it upsets you."

Mo sat on the four poster bed. "I'm not upset." He thought of trying to explain some of his feelings, but didn't. Just like he hadn't managed to talk to her about the events of the last few days, or about Paolo's demand. He didn't know why. After all, she was going to be his wife. Aside from that, he'd been with Julia on and off for the best part of thirteen years. She knew his sensitivity, had played on it quite a few times during their "wars", so he should be able to confide in her... But Mo didn't want to cloud her happiness at the approaching wedding with his inner troubles, even less with the crazy money claim from Paolo. He was the one who would have to deal with the problems.

91

Still, although she was caught in the whirlwind of preparations for the big day, Julia could see her soon-to-be husband wasn't exactly delirious with happiness. "Look, Mo — what's done is done. There's no use dwelling on it," she said.

Mo caught himself remembering her father using more or less the same words thirteen years previously, at that first "family meeting".

"I know you're right. Don't worry, I'll be fine."

Julia got up and came to sit on the bed with him. Her left arm encircled his waist. "It's bad luck to be sad before your wedding... Don't you want to get married any more?" she asked with her little-girl inflection, the one she was so good at using. Her head leaned on his chest.

"No, it's not that... I'm ready — let's get married." He smiled.

"Well, don't think too much about the past. It's over. There's nothing we can do about it." She moved closer, spoke even more softly. "Remember what we said: 'No looking back'."

Mo remembered the motto they had decided to adopt when they got back together on his return. "No looking back," he repeated, not very convincingly.

Julia's hand slipped through the opening in his shirt. "Not even a little glance..."

Mo's eyes caught hers. "OK, not even that," he said, squeezing her uncovered brown thigh.

Julia made a muffled sound, inhaling air between her teeth, that way she had of doing it... Mo felt her fingers clutch at his skin under the shirt. Then she said, "Don't mess about, Mo; I'm late as it is."

Like it was his fault...

Julia stood up and got back to her make-up. Mo watched her for a few seconds. She was a little older, a little rounder, but the woman still could make almost any man turn his head on the street. And he, Mo, was about, finally, to be her lawful wedded husband, as they say.

He got up and started out.

"So, you're gonna be in tonight?" she asked.

"Yeah. I've got to make a call," he said, going down the stairs.

• P E R F E C T   F I T ! •

"You better come check me…" Baloo had been his usual laconic self on the phone.

In the taxi Mo had automatically guessed the likely motive for the call; something had come up about Sam. He paid the driver and walked to the back of the house, where some stairs led to the basement studio. A skinny teenager with a thin first moustache came to open the door. Mo didn't know him, but he must have known Mo as he took the toothpick out of his mouth long enough to smile and greet him.

Downstairs, Baloo sat behind the mixing desk, his big frame leaning slightly forward as he carefully operated the controls. He glanced at Mo through the glass and continued working. The sound was pushy, dry and heavy.

Mo and the youngster entered the small room. Mo took one of the seats at the back; he knew only too well how much undiluted attention mixing required, and was prepared to wait. But he had hardly picked up a music magazine before

Baloo turned and said, "Wha'ppen? Denise wan' see you, you know... upstairs."

"Yeah?" Mo enquired, but Baloo was already back to his task.

Mo got up. Denise... Well, she'd been out the last time he'd come, so she must have sent for him now. Baloo's wife had been like a big sister to him when he'd started hanging around the studio as a teenager. Mo liked Denise a lot, trusted her, and she had never let him down. She was one of these people whose goodness etches a groove in your heart.

Mo climbed back upstairs. At the front door he didn't have to wait long. Still round and brown and warm, Denise pulled him to her and hugged him.

"Lord, Mo... you lose weight!" she exclaimed.

"Yes, Denise, a little — but you still look great!" Mo said.

She laughed. "Still fat... I like your beard, though."

"So... you turn Rasta too?" Mo slipped into his "Yard" accent, pointing to her plaited dread-like hairstyle.

"How you mean? You know seh me ina the Rasta business from dem time deh..."

Mo smiled as she closed the door and led him through to the living room. The woman sitting in front of the television had glasses on and a purple and white top and skirt.

"You know my cousin Pearl, Mo..."

It wasn't a question. Mo recalled Pearl, yes, but it had never really registered that she was Denise's cousin. He'd never seen her at the house. Then another fact hit him and he knew...

"Hi, Pearl, how you doing?" he said.

"Fine, thank you." Her voice was pitched higher than Denise's, almost fluttering.

"Have a seat, Mo... You want a drink?" Denise asked.

Mo sat. "No. I'm all right."

Some Saturday afternoon game show was on, but Pearl seemed to be looking more towards Mo from behind her glasses. They hadn't really known each other, only known of each other. Pearl was one of those people you grow up in the same neighbourhood with, go to the same school and have common acquaintances, but somehow never make it to personal friendship. Then again she was, as far as Mo could now recall, never very extrovert, rather shy in fact, but an excellent student who never attended the hot parties that some of the more "carefree" girls did. Pearl Livingston! Mo's memory for names had always been pretty good. Years later, of course, she'd become Mrs Sousay...

"So, how things, sah?" Denise asked him. She had joined him on the settee, seeming pleased to see him judging by the way her almond eyes crissed.

"Not too bad. Just trying to settle down, you know."

Denise made small talk with him for a while, asking about his travels, getting him to talk about India where he had spent a few months the previous year, and about his mother in Canada.

Pearl was listening, watching Mo most of the time. Inside, he was wondering what she was thinking. His sharp mind had already picked up on the fact that her presence here was no coincidence.

Mo satisfied Denise's curiosity, knowing all the while that this wasn't what he was here for. He knew her well enough to see she was simply delaying the serious talk.

After a short trip to her kitchen, where she said she was boiling some fish soup, Denise said, "So... I hear seh you getting married..."

Pearl turned from the screen to look directly at him.

"Yeah..." Mo nodded slowly. "I told Baloo you and him should come down."

The quick glance between the two women wasn't lost on Mo, but he couldn't guess the meaning of it until Denise asked, "Tell me something, Mo, you sure you know what you doing?"

Denise was turned towards him on the settee, her eyes intent. She was one of the people Mo truly respected. Her tone of voice showed real concern, so the question reached him.

"Well, I've got to settle down now, you know what I mean, Denise? For the children and everything..." He looked at her closely. "Why?"

Denise took time to think about what she wanted to say, which was a sure sign of gravity with her, Mo knew that. She was a highly emotional person, strong but deeply sensitive. "It's a long time I don't see you, Mo, but I want you to know I always prayed for you still, I know seh you would come back..."

Mo smiled a little, nodded to show her he understood.

"You see, you..." Denise hesitated. "You and Sammy... I love you like my little bredda dem, you know that..."

"I know, Denise, and I'll always be thankful for that," Mo told her. Next to his mother he loved Denise, who'd been constant in her care and support. And he knew Sammy could have said the same thing.

"That is why I want you to listen carefully to what you gonna hear, because I will never let nobody hurt you, you better know that!" She gave Mo her silent stare, and he shifted his position a little to sit further back on the settee.

Denise sounded serious, and because of the presence of the silently watchful Pearl, Mo guessed this had to be about the "situation" with Paolo. "Don't worry, Denise; I'm gonna sort out this thing," he said. He felt a little embarrassed to hear that Denise was prepared to stand up for him, and the presence of Pearl made it awkward somehow, especially because she hadn't said a word. Mo looked at her straight for the first time since he had sat down. She wasn't expressing much, just watching and listening in a detached kind of way.

"So, what gonna happen?" he heard Denise ask.

Mo sighed, took his time before replying. "This is a... misunderstanding."

He felt increasingly uncomfortable to be sitting across from the woman whose husband his brother had shot. That was it. That was why he really didn't want to discuss his problem with Denise right now. She should have been able to guess it...

Now Pearl spoke for the first time. "I asked Denise to call you, Mo."

Mo could read no hostility in her eyes. Slowly, he inhaled and told her, "I'm sorry about your husband, Pearl..." Why he had said "husband" instead of naming him, he didn't know.

"Thank you..." Pearl said, then just as Mo was about to say something else she spoke again, as though finishing her sentence: "... and I'm sorry about your brother too."

This Mo found very embarrassing. He glanced at Denise but she had fallen silent.

Pearl adjusted her glasses with a finger upon which gleamed a pretty gold and diamond ring. "Look, Mo..." she started, "I know you had

99

nothing to do with what happened... And I don't usually meddle in people's business, but I wanted to talk to you because you should know, I think..."

You should know... Mo knew that he should know. It was what several people kept inferring: that he should know. But the last few weeks had made him realise precisely that he didn't know what he should know. And since he had been set up to pay back thirty-five grand for something he knew nothing about... well, he had to know. He waited. Pearl seemed to have a lot to say.

"Paolo came to ask you to pay back some money..." It wasn't really a question; Mo could detect the fact that Denise had told her.

He nodded. "Thirty-five grand. He said my brother robbed the business money."

"The business money..." Pearl repeated slowly, her slender hands crossed in her lap. She seemed absorbed for an instant before speaking again. "My late husband, Fitzroy, was a bad man," she said without any particular colour to the statement. "I knew what he did for a living — and I don't make no apologies for being with him. He was the only man I ever been with."

Mo began to wonder if he should be privy to such information. Still, Pearl was airing her soul. "I met him when I was seventeen, got pregnant at eighteen. But Fitzroy married me, looked after me and the three boys for as long as he was alive, and he never mistreated me. I heard what he was like on the street, but I never, ever felt the weight of his hand. Over the years I tried to make him change, make him stop from dealing drugs and everything..." She spoke calmly, her accent showing a hint of the East London of her childhood. "Believe me, Mo, I tried — but he thought that was the only way not to be poor; that was all he knew to make his money. All his family is into that. Fitzroy was a weak man, he couldn't change. That wasn't what I left him for..."

"You left him?" Mo asked, surprised.

Pearl nodded gravely. "I did. A year before he... passed away, I took my boys and moved out. That was when I found out a lot of the things I didn't know about him. Because he was trying to get me to come back, he told me everything... well, a lot of things I didn't know about him."

Mo was attentive; he knew that what he needed to know was somewhere in Pearl's memory, and she was about to let it out.

Denise left to check on her fish soup.

"He shouldn't have robbed your shop," Pearl said disapprovingly. She looked almost as if the blame for the wrongdoing somehow extended to her.

"He told you that?" Mo asked her.

Pearl nodded. "Yes, he did."

That was it — a witness! Mo knew he must push her further, to clear his mind of all doubt. "Was Paolo involved?"

101

But Pearl said, "I don't know for sure," then added somberly: "They were always in everything together anyway..."

This was one established fact anyway in his plan to dismiss Paolo's claim. Pearl looked at Denise, who had been standing in the doorway, listening to her intently. Once again there was that brief eye contact between them.

"Did you know someone set you up for that robbery?" Pearl asked.

The insurance company at the time certainly seemed to think so... "Did Fitzroy tell you who it was?" Mo asked, after reflecting a little on the information.

Pearl inhaled slowly, made a face, and said rather cryptically, "In his last few months, he told me a lot of things..." And for a moment, the woman seemed lost in an inner contemplation.

Denise went to switch off the fire under her pot, came back. There was silence, a pregnant silence spoiled only by the buzzing of the television on low volume. Then, Denise asked Mo, "You remember what I said to you when the robbery happen?"

Mo remembered. Denise had been adamant that only someone close to him and wanting to hurt him could have known certain details to undertake the robbery on the day of the monthly supply of merchandise. For a while Mo had even wondered if Sam wasn't behind it. He asked Pearl, "Was it my brother?"

This time Denise asked, "Where was you living them time deh?"

Mo frowned, tracking back to 1986. "I was living here!"

"You 'member why?"

Sure he did! Julia had just kicked him out of "her" council flat after one of her unfounded jealousy attacks. Mo had preferred use one of Baloo's spare rooms than return to his mother and her I-told-me-so jibes...

"Who you think set you up, Mo?" Denise asked, fixing him with her warm slanted eyes.

Pearl was looking at him too, with what seemed like anticipated embarrassment.

Mo looked slowly from one to the other. He was intelligent enough to see where Denise was getting to... but she had to be wrong. Frowning, he said, "No, Denise... I know what you're thinking, but you're wrong."

He knew Denise had never liked Julia for some reason, but that was going too far, surely. Yet, across the room from him, Pearl's face was grim. He interrogated her with his eyes, and she didn't flinch He shook his head. They had to be wrong. He was thinking back now to that time, the fight with Julia and his six months at Baloo's, his short relationship with Patricia... He quickly dismissed that name out of his mind.

"Pearl, what did Fitzroy say?" he asked, his head empty as he waited for the answer.

"Do you want to know why I left Fitzroy, Mo?" she asked instead.

Mo didn't answer; she wasn't waiting for him to do so anyway. "Because he lied to me," she said with a voice through which emotion filtered. "I loved Fitzroy, and I believe he loved me, in his own way. Ten years ago I had a dream one night, and the next morning I asked him a question and he said no. The year before he died, he came to me and told me he couldn't hold it any longer; he had lied to me all those years before."

Inside his head, Mo could feel the jumbling of thoughts, round and round, leading him to one simple fact he kept refusing to formulate coherently.

"Fitzroy swore to me, to the day of his death, it was just a one-night fling... but he got caught."

Mo looked at Denise then back to Pearl, and felt his body stiffen. It was Denise's hand on his wrist which brought the jabbing pain in his chest. He heard himself asking: "What are you saying?"

Pearl sighed heavily. Mo felt Denise closer to him on the settee. Her arm slid through his while she looked at her cousin, encouraging her to go on. As Pearl continued to explain, Mo listened with an ice cube in his gut.

"I'm sorry, Mo," Pearl said when she'd finished. "I know this must hurt you, but it's the truth. God is my witness."

Never in his life had Mo felt like he did that afternoon leaving Baloo's house. Denise had insisted he eat some of her soup, which as always was delicious, but Mo had hardly tasted anything. Downstairs, Baloo had tried to take his mind off things and offer him some tracks to work on, but he had quickly seen that Mo's mind wasn't there with him. And Mo had left, the wedding invitation he had brought still in his pocket.

Walking though the Stoke Newington back streets, hands deep in the pockets of his jeans, Mo didn't really see anyone or anything around him; but on a screen in his mind rolled sequences of events, images translating the extraordinary story Pearl had just told him, over and over again. It was the kind of plot that, if you saw it in a movie, you'd marvel at its cunning, delight in or shake your head at the deviousness of the characters involved. But in his zombie-like state, slowly heading he wasn't sure where, Mo was in no condition to appreciate such artistic subtleties. The story he'd just heard was a nightmare, his nightmare, the horror of which he was feeling sink deep into the heart of his being. Under the blue skies of a peaceful Saturday afternoon, Mo was sinking emotionally.

"I was with her in primary school; she was a very spiteful girl then..." Pearl had told him afterwards, as if it would be of any comfort to him!

He turned up on Church Street, absentmindedly, but there was too much activity there, too many people. He needed silence, no noise, no one around. He found himself wishing it were night, not a busy afternoon, when he had to contemplate his shame, his embarrassment, in broad daylight.

Another thought sprang up, something Aunt Alda always liked to repeat: "What's in the darkness must be revealed to light." Aunt Alda... She couldn't have known, surely... Yet her dislike of Julia had been spontaneous and constant. Mo could hear a voice asking in his mind: "Who knows about all this? How many people knew all along?" Funny, the part pride plays in human suffering.

Clissold Park held its usual share of mothers and young children, and Mo felt himself drawn across the road. Inside, he passed by the pond, where half-naked toddlers splashed under the benevolent eyes of their chattering mothers. Everything he saw around him started to remind him of his life — what he thought was his life anyway, before...

Mo had been gone from Baloo's house about an hour, and the truth had not really sunk in that deep yet (although he didn't realise it). Certain truths are too horrible to accept when told. Some people refuse to believe in a loved one's death because they never actually saw the lifeless body...

Mo sat on one of the more remote benches, far enough from anyone, knowing his conscious acceptance of what he had been told could not happen until he had heard it from Julia. Quickly repressed memories flooded his mind for a short and painful second, memories of a sweltering summer night with Julia, in this very park, on a bench just like this one, at the dawn of their story...

His back against the wood, head tilted upwards to the cruelly smiling skies above, Mo tried to dismiss as hearsay and unsubstantiated allegations these incredible accusations, like a skilful barrister derisively thrashing the prosecution's argument to bits. But it all fitted so well together, Pearl's story.

Slowly, he went through the elements of the plot one by one, checking each detail carefully with what he knew to be true. The more he did so, the less he was managing to loosen up the steely fingers clawing at his stomach. He felt pain, physical pain, as his mind wrestled with his heart inside him. How could it be true? How could a woman he had known for so many years and been through so much with turn out to be the vicious, scheming character he had just heard about? It was impossible. They had to be wrong! Mo wanted to refute the very facts he had been given because his heart could not accept that, despite their numerous break-ups, fall-outs and fights, Julia could ever have betrayed him. For betrayed was really what Mo felt this afternoon: betrayed by his woman, betrayed by his sense of right and wrong, of reality and fiction, betrayed by life.

He remained seated there for some time, oblivious even to the glorious sunset, prey to the demons that lurked, ready to enter him once the reaction properly set in.

It was not until after eleven that Mo got home, having walked aimlessly around. He knew he would be alone. He didn't want to be here, wanted neither food nor sleep to comfort him. In the empty house he sat, in the dark, awake, until only disgust remained at the inner core of his being. Finally he went to bed and surrendered to the smooth embrace of sleep

Mo woke up to sneaky rays of sunshine through the drawn blinds and the warmth of a slumbering form next to him. Anyone who has ever gone to sleep after a painful experience knows just how fast the conscious mind sets in upon awaking. Mo slid out of the bed and out of the bedroom right away.

After an argument or a fight, you can always make up the next day and forget about it; or if you really feel bad, you'll go away and let time pass, for a couple of days anyway, before the reconciliation. But here there was no such way. Mo wished he had it in himself to drag the woman upstairs out of her contented sleep and confront her. But he had no idea what time she had come into the bed after her presumably enjoyable "hen party", so instead he showered, ate an orange downstairs, then purposefully went to fetch the heavy punching bag from the cellar.

Left jab — right uppercut — right hook... Quick stance switch... Right block — right thrust punch — low left kick — right elbow slap...

Mo shuffled on the spot and slid into two more fast combinations, smooth, accurate, his jaws clenched hard as he unleashed the punches into the sand-filled bag. Through his nose the breath came out in short bursts, punctuating the blows; he could feel rivulets of sweat dripping slowly from his forehead on to his nose and cheeks. Eyes focused, Mo ignored the Sunday morning rising sun, pretty and bright, and exhaled deeply, channelling out the air through the centre of his body as he had been taught. It had been some years since he'd properly trained, and after twenty minutes on the heavy bag he could already feel the strain in his shoulder muscles. His stamina was lesser than it had been back then, but the technique was still there, he realised. Years spent practising the various patterns of the fighting system had imprinted them deeply into his subconscious. It was like his teacher had always insisted: when switched on, the system takes over your body.

Mo stepped back from the bag, his arms hanging loosely by his sides. Breathing deeply in and out, he let his chest fill with air, calming down his rhythm. As the pain in his bruised knuckles started to kick in, he realised he should have gone to look for his gloves.

Yeah — he still possessed the skills; he could still "explode", as his teacher used to say. The way he felt this morning, Mo found that part came easily...

At the waterhose Mo wet his parched throat, splashed his sweaty face. He ran the water over his aching knuckles, then switched off the tap and went in. The carton of apple juice in the fridge offered only enough to make him more thirsty, and the mineral water was finished. Mo decided he'd better get to the shop.

While he got his breath back he sat at the kitchen table, trying to study the review section of the Sunday paper. Then he saw Julia's feet coming down the stairs. In a T-shirt, with strands of hair pointing every which way, she seemed half-asleep.

"All right? You mind picking up the kids from Mum's for me? I'm late to go to Wembley market with Felicia..."

Mo looked up slowly from his paper, wishing he didn't have to. He realised he didn't even know what he wanted to say.

Julia was switching on the kettle. "I have such a headache..." she said, then frowned. "What's the matter with you?"

"I'd like to ask you something," Mo said.

His voice must have sounded strange; he saw Julia's inquisitive stare and turned his eyes away first. So many things had been going through his mind when he'd woken up earlier on, yet now only a resigned weariness remained. The punishing workout had sapped the surplus energy in his body and stilled the tumult in his heart. He said, "You remember Pearl Livingston?"

Julia poured hot water out of the kettle on to the tea bag in her mug. "Pearl Livingston?" she repeated.

Mo was watching her. "Yeah... She was in the same class as you in primary."

"That's going back a long way..." Julia remarked.

"I met her yesterday," Mo said calmly.

He waited. Julia knew who he was talking about, and she knew the reason he was mentioning that name this morning; Mo was sure of it. He watched her sip a little of the tea. Standing barefoot at the breakfast bar, she seemed fully awake now.

"How is she?"

If she felt in any way worried by the mention of Pearl, Julia's voice didn't show it. Mo reflected to himself once again that he didn't have any actual proof of what he was going to say, only Pearl's word.

Sighing, he crossed his hands over the table top. "Not too bad... for a widow."

111

Their eyes met across the divide, then Julia shifted hers away and slowly put the mug down on the bench. Her arms crossed over her chest. She looked at Mo again, then away. "What did she say?" Now her voice came out somewhat lower.

"Where d'you want me to start?" Mo asked.

So it was all true. Mo knew Julia enough to see her nervousness; perhaps she wasn't such a consummate actress after all... The silence lasted maybe a full minute. An almost palpable chill hung over the sunlit kitchen.

Julia still wasn't saying anything, her gaze switching from Mo at the table to the tall fridge-freezer in the corner.

"I just want to know one thing," Mo told her. She wasn't looking in his direction as he continued: "Did you get together with Fitzroy before or after the robbery?"

The hard question jerked Julia out of her mutism. Her hands went to her face and she said in a broken tone, "It's not like it seems, Mo. Please..."

"No 'please'. And no crying either..."

Mo put his hands flat on the table, knowing how easy tears could spring from her eyes. He paused to control his voice, keeping his cold anger in check. "Look. I just want to know."

Julia's hands were clasped together. "You left me for that girl. I... I was hurt. I didn't really mean for all that to happen," she said feebly.

"No?" Mo smirked. "What did you mean to happen? Tell me! Which part of it?"

"It wasn't like that, Mo... You've got to believe me," Julia pleaded, real tears now in her brown eyes.

It was the word "believe", maybe more than the apparent weakness, that infuriated Mo. Now she was acting meek, playing him for a fool once again. He didn't realise his brain was given such an order, but one moment the glass fruit bowl was in the centre of the table, and the next, Mo's forearm had swept it off and sent it crashing against the wall.

The sound of breaking glass made Julia jump back along the bench a good yard. Her whole body tensed at the unexpected violence. In all the years they had been together, Mo had never raised his hand to her, despite everything she had put him through. Indeed, quite a few people would have argued that, at some point, someone should have done her a big favour by straightening up Julia Kline's head with a sound beating.

Mo inhaled deeply and pointed his index at her sternly. "I have to believe you?! Is that what you say?"

He stared at her and, maybe for the first time since she'd met him, Julia felt fear. She could read the edge in his stony stare.

Mo wasn't finished. "I have believed in you — for twelve years, fool that I was — and that's what got me where I am today. Everybody knew you were a snake, it seems, except me."

Julia's head was down, tears in full flow.

Mo said with a blank voice, "I'm gonna ask you one more time: Fitzroy... was it before or after the robbery?" He knew she understood exactly the implications, whichever way she would answer.

Finally she said in a low tone, "Before."

"Right... So you threatened to tell his wife if he didn't do what you wanted?"

Julia looked up at him briefly. "I didn't. He said he would make sure you found out unless I gave him some information..."

"That's not what he told his wife!"

"It's true!"

Mo nodded and sneered. "Yeah? But you made him pay you for years, didn't you? So who blackmailed who? I want to know..."

Julia stood in the corner, her eyes to the floor. Mo heard her say, "It only happened once... I didn't mean to go with him, I don't know what happened..."

Mo almost laughed despite himself. "Well, only two people do know, and one of them is dead..."

"It's true. He spiked my drink in the club that night. I don't remember what happened... That's why I made him pay."

Their eyes met briefly, but Julia wasn't into visual contact today.

Mo sat back in the chair. He felt extremely weary, emotionally drained. The whole story was leaving him with a bitter taste. "You sure?" he asked.

This time Julia lifted her head for more than a few seconds, and Mo felt her searching gaze. He could have sworn he caught a glimpse of something akin to bewilderment crossing her strained features.

"What do you mean?"

Mo took his time, the pause adding weight to the direct question. "That money Fitzroy was paying you — was it to support his child?"

Thick tension. Julia's anguished face spoke louder than words.

"Pearl told you that?" she asked in a shaky voice.

"It took seven years, but Fitzroy cracked and told her," Mo said. Adding sadly, "No more money..."

The game was up. Julia took refuge in a few seconds of silence before speaking again. "I lied to Fitzroy."

Now it was Mo's turn to be quiet while in his mind the counter-information found its place in the tortuous scheme he had unravelled. What was she talking about now? "What?"

Julia insisted. "I made him believe the child was his. I lied..."

How candid an admission from a woman like Julia! Mo frowned. He had felt so thoroughly confused since the previous afternoon that he now found some relief in knowing the whole truth. Doubt, especially about this particular element of the story, he could not bear. He had to know.

"Is there nothing sacred to you? Don't you respect anything, not even your own child?" he asked, genuinely horrified.

But Julia was unrepentant. "I lied to him, he believed me — and that's why he kept on paying," she added, finishing with what sounded like a tearfully honest plea. "Vinny is your son; you know that, Mo!"

"Do I?" He glared at the woman. "Do I really?" He slammed the palm of his hand on the wooden table top. "All I know is that Vinny was born the same year I got back with you." He paused to let his fury subside, then waited to catch Julia's eyes before telling her, "I also know it was the same year my shop got robbed..."

He stood up, shook his head. Disgust was what he felt inside, deep loathing for the woman he had thought he knew and loved, despite everything. Today, he realised that all certainty about the last twelve years with this woman had gone for ever. Everything, down to the paternity of the children she had borne, had become shaky ground.

"You don't even know yourself, do you?" he said bitterly, then turned away and walked upstairs.

Surviving an accident is one thing, making it through the long wait in the casualty department of a hospital is quite another.

Mo watched the two white men in work clothes sitting opposite him. The one with the Bloody bandage around his head was about as hurt as anyone can be without being unconscious on a stretcher, but he had been waiting at least an hour. The population of the waiting room offered just about anything in terms of wounds and bruises one can think of. Maybe Friday morning was a particularly accident-prone time, Mo thought, or maybe it was like this every day. He didn't know, but he wished Vinny hadn't cut his hand at such a peak hour.

Beside him on the plastic chair, the young boy with the wrapped-up left hand surveyed the congregation of his fellow victims with a knitted brow.

"You OK?" Mo asked him.

Vinny nodded without changing expression. "I'm not gonna have to go to the barber, am I?"

117

It was the second time since they'd arrived that Vinny had asked. Here was this kid, an inch-long cut in the middle of his hand, and all he's concerned about is his hairstyle!

Mo smiled resignedly and shook his head. "Don't worry about it."

The man to the left of Vinny with his arm in a sling moved to the next seat, so they got up and moved too. One step further. Vinny was going to need some stitches. The large knife he had tried cutting a loaf of bread with could just as well have sliced off one of his fingers! Vinny's attempt at making toast for breakfast had gotten him this far. Mo didn't blame him, he just didn't like all this waiting. The way Vinny's hand had looked when Mo got to the kitchen earlier on, he had not had time to think of packing a book.

Mo had planned on spending the morning hours at the gym, working out a little, but that was out of the question now. Just like children to come up with unexpected activities for you. But this queuing was really taking too long, and with the summer still blooming strong every day, the atmosphere in the casualty department was getting kind of stifling.

Mo asked Vinny, "You want a drink?"

"All right."

Mo got up. "You wait here and keep the line; I'll be right back."

118

Mo left his son and stepped out. He wasn't worried about Vinny. The boy was more than able to take care of himself; he was no simpleton.

The hospital was a new experience to Mo. He remembered being taken to the old casualty department at Homerton with a broken finger as a youngster, but this was all modern-style: clean and very busy. The main hall looked like a train station, the way people were shifting around, getting directions and heading towards the upper floors with bags in their hands and various looks on their faces. A large Turkish-looking woman who brushed past Mo's shoulder single-mindedly might have had a sister or even a daughter having her first baby somewhere upstairs. That younger man, on the other hand, walking towards the exit in such a brow-beaten manner, seemed under the weight of a heavy burden...

Mo found the drinks machine short on choice but relatively low-priced. He got out two Cokes. He turned around and started out and almost got run over by a thin, tall young woman in white, involved in a hundred-yard dash, it seemed, from the way she was sprinting towards the other end of the hall.

"Sorry..." she still found time to say as she spun around to avoid him. But then she stopped, and he frowned, because she was frowning.

"Mo... It's Mo, ain't it?"

Mo squinted, not quite making out the face.

But she knew him, she was sure now, and she smiled, her full eyes enjoying his puzzlement. "It's me — Marian..."

"Marian?" Mo repeated, trying his best — but he just wasn't there yet.

The slim girl was still smiling. "Marian. Angie's sister."

"Marian!" Mo said incredulously, scrutinising her face. Now he knew. She had Angie's eyes! They were sisters — you could tell by looks alone — but the Marian he remembered was a skinny kid of twelve. The girl in front of him was as tall as him, wearing white dungarees and a very tight-fitting vest... kind of see-through. "Marian?" Mo said again. "What happened?"

She laughed, showing perfect white teeth and a gold one near the middle. "I'm all right... What are you doing here?" she asked

"I have my boy in casualty. He cut his hand... What about you? Where were you running to like that?"

Marian stopped smiling, recalling why she was there. "Angie's in here, you know!"

"What? But... I saw her recently; she said she had another couple of months..."

"She was having contractions. She left a message on the answerphone... Look, I've got to go." She turned to run.

Mo called out, "Which ward?"

The girl spun around and shouted, "Priestley!"

"I'm gonna check her!" Mo said, but she was already out of sight.

He returned to casualty, where Vinny was a few seats closer to deliverance. It still took them another twenty-five minutes to be seen to. Once he had been stitched up (which he endured bravely) and bandaged, Vinny looked none the worse for wear and was already talking about his Sunday football match.

Mo took him to look for Angie. They found her sitting in bed, eating grapes, looking quite fresh. Mo smiled and shook his head. "You scared your sister to death!"

Marian smiled at him.

Angie said, "It's nice to know people care. Why you never come look for me, Mo?"

Mo apologised. "I meant to come, really! I been busy, you know..."

"Yeah, I know," she said. "Is that Vinny?"

"That's him!"

Vinny made a face and said "Hi".

"Hi, Vinny! What happened to your hand?" Angie asked.

"Got cut," he said simply.

"What did the doctor say?" Mo asked Angie.

"He said it might be a false alarm. I hope it is!"

"You don't feel anything?"

"I had some pains early this morning." Angie shrugged. "But now I feel fine." Then she pushed another grape in her mouth. She didn't look ready to have this baby yet.

121

Mo asked, "They're sending you home?"

"I'm not staying here! I'm just waiting for the doctor to come back." Angie handed the empty plate to her sister and got out of bed slowly, belly first.

"Where you going?" Marian asked. She still looked concerned about her sister's condition. But Angie already had her slippers on and was pulling on her dressing gown.

"I need to walk. Come, Mo," she said.

Mo let her rest her hand on his arm. "Vin, I soon come, all right?"

Vinny was all right.

Angie and Mo took time walking towards the end of the corridor. "Sometimes you feel better walking than sitting down," Angie said, adding hopefully, "I can't wait for this baby to come!"

Mo laughed. "And he knows that. That's why you're getting some pain already — he's upset with you."

Angie smiled and breathed deeply.

"You OK?" Mo asked her.

She nodded. "I'm fine."

Though she might have been little in size, Angie was as tough as they come. Mo had always had respect for her.

She asked him, "How's everything?"

Mo could feel her eyes watching his face carefully. He found himself wondering what she knew. (In fact, for most of the week he had been wondering on and off exactly who knew what of the story he had come across so suddenly the previous weekend.) "Rough, to tell you the truth," he said quite honestly.

They were standing near the doors at the end of the corridor. Angie asked, "You're still getting married?"

Mo sighed, pausing under the scrutinising eyes of the small woman with the large stomach. "I'm gonna do it for the children," he told her, and got a deep, meaningful stare in return.

He sighed again. This had surely been the most torturing week of his entire life. After the Sunday morning confrontation with Julia, he had kept a very low profile in and out of the house. He needed time to think things over, and Julia's guilt-ridden and tearful pleas to him had made it even worse. Mo had felt gutted that evening, lower than he'd ever been, as he tried to hang on to his sanity while dealing with the re-emergence of his brother's memory — on top of the awful revelations from his wife-to-be. All day he had been out, at the park, where he'd spent hours around the banks of the pond. When it started to get dark he'd dialled Carmen's number, but had hung up as the phone started to ring at the other end. He hadn't even managed to tell her he was getting married; no way he could come up with that now. No, he couldn't see Carmen.

So he'd gone to Baloo's studio, and as expected Baloo hadn't asked him anything; he'd just carried on with what he was doing and let Mo hang around the back by himself. Mo had slept upstairs at the studio that night.

The next day, Mo had had to endure the supplication of a seemingly contrite Julia, and he didn't enjoy that. From naivety to cynicism, the change in Mo's outlook had been rapid. With Julia literally begging forgiveness and the children sensing something major was going down, Mo had had an extremely unpleasant week.

He put his hand on Angie's shoulder. "There's nothing I can do about it now, Ange; either I take care of business or I turn my back on the children and run. You know what I mean?"

Angie shook her head sadly.

Mo said, "Look, Angie, I know this is not the right time to bother you with this type of thing, but could I ask you just one question?"

"Come on, Mo," she said, "what is it?"

Mo waited a little, then asked her, "Did Sam come to your place that night, the last night..." He felt bad saying it like that.

Angie looked seriously at him. "No. And it's just as well, because Fitzroy's brothers came looking for him."

"What?"

Angie nodded. "Yeah, they turned my place upside down."

"They shook you up?" Mo asked.

"No, they just searched everywhere, looking for some money. But I told them I hadn't seen

Sam in three weeks. Then the police came as well. I didn't even know what was going on! It was rough, Mo..."

"Look, I'm sorry to bring this back..."

Angie shrugged. "It's all right now. It's been three years and I've learned to deal with it..." She paused as though thinking of something. "You know, Mo, Sammy was trying to get clean in the last few months. He told me he was, and I believe he was telling the truth... I really loved him."

The way she'd spoken the last sentence touched Mo. Despite his brother's ways, he knew Sam had loved her too.

"How did Sam find out... about Fitzroy?" Mo asked her straight.

Angie shook her head. "I don't know. He came to see me one night, the week before he died. He looked well vexed..."

Mo was listening intently.

"I hadn't seen him for a while before that. You know how he moved around a lot," Angie said as an aside before continuing. "I gave him some food and later he told me the story. He was really upset. He stayed the night, and I didn't see him or hear from him again, until that night..."

Mo looked straight at Angie. "He called you?"

Angie nodded gravely.

"Where was he?"

"I don't know," Angie answered, "but he was crying."

"Crying?"

Angie's face showed her love for Sam still lived on. "He called just after the police had left. He sounded well upset, crying and talking about you..."

Mo felt the little tug in his chest. "What did he say?"

"He was in a cabin somewhere... He kept saying, 'I done Mo wrong', something like that. He got cut off... didn't call back."

Mo absentmindedly squeezed Angie's arm. He could feel emotion welling inside him, like he had just heard his brother's voice from beyond. But what did Sam mean by that?

"Anyway, don't dwell on that too much, Mo," Angie told him. "Grief can destroy people. We're alive, and we've got to cope."

And she was right. Mo walked her back down to the ward. He wrote down her home phone number and promised he would call later that evening. Then he and Vinny left the hospital.

"Why have I got to go to Grandma's? It's boring down there..."

Mo glanced at Vinny's closed features and asked deviously, "You'd prefer to come to the barber's with me?" He knew full well that would make up Vinny's mind fast.

"What time is Mum picking me up?" the boy asked, not bothering to answer Mo's question.

"She said around two."

126

They had just left McDonald's, where Mo had bought lunch for the wounded Vinny. He had to drop him off as arranged before making the few moves he had planned.

When they got to the estate, Vinny's grandfather opened the door for them. His wife had gone "down the road" and would be back soon, he said. Mo and Vinny sat on the settee in front of the TV.

A pair of glasses on top of his nose, Mr Kline was busy filling betting slips that were scattered over the living room table. "You buy horses?" he asked Mo.

"Not really, you know. I don't have no luck in gambling."

That was true. And Mo knew nothing about horses, either. The two occasions when he had tried it, years ago, when many of his teenage friends had started their 'bookie' operations, he had lost, and had never tried again since then. Unlike Sam, who had seemed to know every thoroughbred personally and rarely failed to at least make back his money.

"This one is a sure shot!" Mr Kline said, leaning over the slip as he wrote down his bet. He finished, and gathered his bits of paper and newspapers, looking satisfied with himself. Taking off his glasses, he told Mo, "I'm gonna place them round the corner; I soon come." He slipped on his jacket and left the house.

127

Vinny was immersed in a programme on the screen, so Mo drifted back into his reflections. He felt weary, mentally tired, the stress caused by what he had found out now taking its toll on his body. He hadn't had any proper sleep all week. He'd sleep, but would keep waking up, uncharacteristically, and would end up tired for the rest of the following day. How he wished he could escape all that, just hop on a flight and leave the ugliness of his present position. At least somewhere else he could, after a while, tell himself that it didn't matter, that it was all past and gone. Right now, though it might be past, it was certainly not gone, and Mo had begun to realise that it would never go away, ever. The cause of all the pain was here with him every day, slept beside him in the same bed — and, moreover, would be doing so "till death do us part" after tomorrow.

Tomorrow...

Beside him, Vinny burst out laughing at the antics of one of the characters he was watching. Mo turned his way. The young boy saw and heard nothing around him when he was watching television. He would become totally absorbed in the programmes, especially movies — the worst thing you could do to him was to interrupt him then.

Mo caught himself scrutinising Vinny's face again. He felt bad doing it, and angry that these suspicions about the boy's parentage could ever

have entered his mind. But he knew that he had
been doing the same thing all week, no matter
how he tried not to. He recalled several instances
when, as a young man, friends of his had had to
face that kind of thing. Stories about "jackets", as
they were popularly called, were commonplace in
the community in which he had grown up. Being
given another man's child as one's own by a
shameless woman was bad enough, Mo thought
— but at least the surrogate father would know
who the real father is! But for him, to realise that
the mother herself didn't really know... that
drove him crazy. The fact that that person would
unscrupulously use the child for her own
advancement and security gave the situation an
even uglier shade.

Look and wonder as he might, Mo was
becoming aware of one thing: he would never be
able to tell. And because Nicole was almost a
replica of himself, Mo had no one to compare
Vinny's features to. Whatever the case, Mo knew
in his heart that he loved the little boy and had
brought him up as his son. And Vinny loved him
as a father, nothing could change that.

So Mo reached the point where it made no
difference any more. These two children were all
he had now; and to be with them, he was about to
marry a woman he could no longer trust...

The front door slammed shut, pulling Mo back
to the present.

"Oh... you're here! How you doing?" Mrs Kline walked in, carrying two plastic bags.

"Fine, thank you," Mo answered.

She dropped her bags and showered her affection on Vinny, who tried to contain his annoyance at being smothered in that way.

"Where's Grandpa?" she asked him.

Vinny shrugged, his attention already back to the screen.

"He's gone to place some bets," Mo told her.

"Always wasting money on horses!" Mrs Kline picked up her bags and disappeared into the kitchen. Less than ten minutes later her husband walked in. Mo nodded to his silent question and decided it was time to take his leave.

"I'm leaving, sir," Mo said. "I have to go to the barber's." He had never called the man anything but "sir".

"I'm leaving too." Indeed, the man seemed to be in a hurry to go. Mo went to say goodbye to his mother-in-law and told Vinny his mother would come for him soon, but the boy didn't care as long as he could watch TV.

Mo and Mr Kline left together. "Where you going?" the man asked as they walked outside. "I'll drop you off."

"It's all right. I'm going to Wood Green, I'll catch a cab."

"Come, I'll drop you off at the cab station then..."

Mo could hardly refuse. He hadn't had that much to do with Julia's father in the past, but still he liked him. He opened the passenger door of the parked Sierra and got in.

"You going to do some shopping?" Mr Kline asked as they eased into the traffic on the main road.

"No, I've got to go to the barber."

"Barber? In Wood Green?"

Mo nodded. "Yeah. I usually go there."

"So, how much him charge you?" Julia's father asked.

"About eight pounds."

"Eight pounds!" Mr Kline stopped at the Hackney Baths traffic lights. "I cut you hair for you, man. For free," he said.

Mo smiled and declined politely, not taking the man seriously — but he was wrong. Mr Kline insisted that Mo should let him cut his hair. After all, he was a bona fide barber with years of experience... "I can do you any style you want, you know — any style!" he told Mo confidently.

And it was convenient too, as he was just on his way to his friend Lester's house, where he usually plied for trade among acquaintances on a Saturday afternoon... So Mo sighed and said "OK", and they drove on together.

Half an hour later, Mo was sitting on a kitchen chair in a flat in Hoxton, where four of Mr Kline's friends had started a noisy game of Dominoes in the living room. The haircut was in progress.

Lester, the resident host, was busy putting the finishing touches to a pot of food he was cooking on the stove. From time to time he took a sip from his glass on the bench nearby. He covered the pan, washed his hands, dried them, and leaned against the sink. He was a short, rotund man with a bushy moustache and greyish hair jutting out from underneath his tweed cap.

"Yes, man. It taking shape already," he commented appreciatively.

Mo wondered exactly what shape it was taking, doubting that Lester and he had the same taste when it came to hairstyles. But Mr Kline seemed to be handling his head very expertly, moving around the chair, stopping, positioning his head at various angles before cutting in lightly with the scissors.

Next door someone exclaimed, "You raas, you!" Another man laughed loudly, a sound as deep as a barrel. Mo suspected that this outburst probably came from the gentle giant with the beard, who had been introduced to him simply as "Junior". Mr Kline's friends had all seemed happy to see him, especially because, as Mo got to understand, they were all coming to the wedding — his wedding. The beer bottles and the quart of rum on the table near them contributed to their buoyant mood, and it was still early afternoon...

"All right," Mr Kline said after a few more minutes of cutting through Mo's hair.

132

Lester downed a little rum from his glass and nodded, smiling at Mo. "This man is not any old barber, you know," he said confidently, "he's an artist."

Mr Kline accepted the compliment modestly. "Thirty-five years I cut heads," he commented, running a comb though Mo's hair and snipping at a few strays.

Mo watched both men nod, wondering how it really looked.

"Bring the mirror, Lester," Mr Kline said.

Lester came back with an oval mirror and held it in front of Mo... It wasn' bad at all, to be honest. Mo's heart settled in his chest. It looked good, in fact.

"Yeah, it looks good," he said.

"Ahhhhh!" Lester exclaimed.

"I do the beard for you," Mr Kline told Mo.

Twenty minutes later, Mo was like new. He took a last look in the mirror, checked his neatly trimmed beard and shapely haircut, and thanked Mr Kline.

"That all right, man." He smiled, then added slyly, "You owe me eight pounds fifty." Then he and Lester laughed at the joke, and Mo smiled too. Lester swept the kitchen floor and the three of them joined the others in the living room. Mo sat beside Lester on the couch while Mr Kline poured himself a drink of rum and went to investigate why his usual partner was losing today.

Junior slammed a card on the table and everything jumped.

The beady-eyed, unshaven man next to him raised his eyebrows and said, "You can mash up the table and everyt'ing in yah, but if you spill my glass me and you will fight." His slurred speech denoted a regular cane juice drinker.

"Shut up and play the right card, Bertie!" his partner called from across the table.

Bertie played — the wrong card apparently. Junior laughed loud and heavy.

The partner cursed. "What happen to you, you drunk?"

That seemed to sting Bertie. With an offended tone he replied, "I never been drunk in my life."

Another thump on the table brought more loud exclamations. To outsiders, the fracas in the room could have been mistaken for the prelude to a fight, but it was all good-humoured; indeed, the longer they played the more liquor they consumed and the louder and happier they all were.

"So this is where he spends his Saturdays," Mo said to himself, watching Mr Kline's relaxed face. He had never seen the man smile much, but he seemed quiet a different person among his friends.

Beside him, Lester said to Mo, "But wait — you don't have a drink!" He got up and made for the table.

"I don't drink," Mo told him.

134

"What you talking about? A man have to have a little drink from time to time..."

Mo had never been a drinker, though he used to enjoy a cold beer or a stout now and then. Strong liquor wasn't his thing in any case. "I haven't even had a beer in three years," he explained to Lester, who was coming back with a bottle of rum and a glass.

From the table, Junior remarked, "You must have been in prison."

"What you taking about!" Bertie cut in. "Is in prison man drink the most."

They laughed.

Lester, meanwhile, had poured out half a glass.

"Seriously — I can't drink that," Mo pleaded.

One of the players, who'd been comparatively quiet up to then, turned to him and said, "Young man, you getting married tomorrow. If you never drink up to now, you better start!"

The whole table erupted in laughter.

"But how you can tell the boy that, Oswald?" Junior said. "After your wife lef' you because you drink rum!"

Quite serious now, Oswald glanced at the big man from behind his glasses. "She said I had to choose: her or the bottle... It was the best decision I ever made."

Roars of laughter around the room.

Bertie's voice came through as the noise died down for a second: "My wife would never leave me because of that." He sounded adamant.

Peter, Bertie's partner at the table, sneered. He scratched his bald pate, played his hand and declared, "Your wife drinks more than you."

Another round of guffaws.

"Card!" Oswald announced.

"Just take your time and sip it," Lester said encouragingly, pushing the glass in Mo's hand. There wasn't much he could do now, so Mo took it. The smell alone went to his head...

"Taste this, man; vintage rum from Barbados. The best!"

Mo would have taken his word for it, but Lester was watching him expectantly, as though waiting for his opinion. He took a sip, a small one. The coolness of the liquid turned rapidly into a fiery arrow in his throat. He coughed.

Lester smiled. "All right!" he said.

Slurring, Bertie addressed the assembly. "That rum saaf, man. We have a rum back home... if you smell it you faint!"

The next fifteen minutes were devoted to a lively debate as to which country produced the strongest rum, with Lester insisting that Barbados rum had no equal, while Bertie asserted that Jamaican country rum was so strong it could make a man sleepwalk. In his corner, Mo was taking time sipping the liquor. Such boasts did nothing to encourage him. Then Mr Kline took Bertie's place and the game went on.

Two hours later the heat had settled in Mo's stomach. There was still rum in his glass but very little, and he had resisted two attempts by Lester to refill it. Bertie, on the other hand, was slumped in a chair, having consumed maybe close to a pint of the stuff, and heckling the players persistently, passing hilarious remarks about whatever topic happened to come around.

Mo was now feeling quite relaxed in the congenial atmosphere. He had all but forgotten about his problem and his impending wedding. He asked Lester: "You do this every week?"

"Except when there's a tournament; this is just practice..."

Soon afterwards, Lester went to the kitchen and proceeded to serve each man a bowl of the stew he had cooked. Everyone welcomed the food — Mo especially, as the strong drink had been tugging at his stomach. He hadn't had much to eat all day.

Fortunately, the hot food tasted delicious. When it was finished more drinks circulated, because, as Junior told Mo: "We drink to get hungry first... then we drink to digest." It sounded logical enough to Mo. He managed to convince Lester he would settle for a beer this time, so he found himself with a large can of Pils to tackle.

He wasn't quite sure what time it was when Bertie said, "Let's go to the pub!"

Mo thought about it. He was by now less than sober, and going to the pub with his present companions could prove fatal. After all, they all had probably thirty years of "practice" over him! He said something about having to go, but his objection was drowned in the chorus of voices insisting he should come along.

"The wedding is tomorrow!" Oswald stated buoyantly. "And since we have the groom with us, we might as well start celebrating now!"

That motion got popular approval and the next thing he knew, Mo was in the back of Sydney's car (as Mr Kline was called by all) between Peter and Bertie; Junior was in the passenger seat. Oswald was driving behind them with Lester.

Weddings and married life were the topics, and the jokes were coming down thick and fast. These men, all of them in their fifties or thereabouts, were "veterans" of the matrimonial state. The sentiments dropping in that car would have given most feminists a seizure.

"I have three daughters," Oswald told Mo as they drove along Kingsland Road, "and let me tell you, I prefer to be their father than their husbands." He laughed at the thought. Peter agreed, stating that — no matter how difficult it had been to find oneself a "good" wife in his days — he felt sorry for the young men of today.

Never short of an anecdote, Bertie explained, "You see, on my wedding day, I was so drunk I had to have two of my friends hold me up in the church. At first the pastor refuse to go though with it. Him say (here Bertie put on a solemn voice): 'You are disgracing the house of the Lord!' " He laughed; so did everyone else in the car. "But everybody tell him to gwan and do it. When him ask me, 'Do you...' this and that, I just nodded. Him ask me again, but that was all I could do. The third time I say 'yes', so him get on wit it same way... I would have never got married sober..." Then he added, deadpan: "And I been drinking ever since, to forget that day."

Peter spoke: "You lucky — your wife all right!"

"All right?!" Bertie looked at him like he was mad.

"Yeah, man. She cool..." Peter insisted. "You see my wife? I been working night shifts for twenty-five years, just so that I only see her on weekend!"

Mo laughed before anybody else.

He heard Mr Kline say, "Oh, so that's why you always do night shifts!" and wondered how bad Peter's wife actually was.

Mr Kline went on: "You know, they have a saying back home..."

Everyone waited expectantly, as everyone loves a saying from "back home".

"They say: 'Before you marry your woman, take a good look at her mother.' "

Bertie, definitely the most irreverent of the group, said, "Good advice, that! So what make you never do that before you marry your wife, then?"

Even in his euphoric state, Mo wondered whether his prospective father-in-law might take slight at the apparent slur on his wife. But he heard him say, "By the time I met my wife, her mother had left for America... I never met the woman till years later..." Loud laughter filled the car.

Mr Kline steered into an empty kerbside space, parked, and they all stumbled out. Outside the pub, a dozen men and women were hanging out on the pavement in the early evening sun, glasses in their hands, chatting. Inside, the bar was lively, with old-time ska music filling the smoky air.

They settled at a double table near the back door. Some continued with rum, some drank beer, and Mo got away with a mere creamy pint of Guinness. He was toasted loudly and with much pomp and ceremony, so that pretty soon even the people standing outside knew he was getting married the following day. But by then he hardly cared any more. His head was light, and on his face there was a little smile of which he was hardly aware, while around him the big men made merry.

Mo was finishing his second pint. Absentmindedly, he observed a police van on the other side of the road, driving slowly past the group of drinkers cooling outside the pub. The first street lamps were on already.

In his mind, amidst the music and the loud voices, he was calculating that, if each man in their group insisted on buying a round, he would have to drink six pints of Guinness, which meant he would be three times as inebriated as he felt now. He wasn't going to survive this!

Just then, one of Julia's brothers showed up at the table. Oliver, or Ollie as everyone called him, already knew his father's drinking habits. He was the youngest of the Kline boys, one year older than Julia. He was also the only one Mo had had a friendship with. His two elder brothers lived out of the area and it was just as well as far as Mo was concerned, for he and they had never been close. On the contrary. He could recall both of them siding with their mother in her efforts to break up his relationship with Julia. The oldest one was some kind of "reverend" in a church, and couldn't start a sentence without saying "The Lord...". And the other one... well, suffice to describe him as a "would-be-middle class, wannabe-white, shallow, coloured guy".

No, Mo didn't care for the two older brothers, but Ollie... Ollie was cool. He lived in Hackney still, worked part-time as a DJ for a radio station, and was down with everything cultural. He seemed to be his father's favourite too, maybe because he looked like him the most.

Ollie grabbed a chair and sat next to Mo at the corner. Right away a drink came down from the bar for him. "What's up, Mo? I didn't know you knew this spot!" he said.

"I didn't. I ain't had a drink for years... I got kidnapped, man!"

Ollie laughed and drank some of his beer. "Dem guys dangerous, I'm telling you!" he said. Then he asked, "So, you ready for tomorrow?"

Mo paused to look at him. Merry as he felt now, he had almost forgotten about it for a while. Alcohol, he realised, has this effect of distancing you from any problem you might wish to forget. "I guess so," he said.

Of course, Ollie didn't know anything about his sister's doings, just like her father, and there was no way Mo would ever talk. That's how he was. He asked Ollie, "How's the music business, man?"

"It's happening, you know. Get some gigs here and there... I got a tune coming out next month — wicked rhythm. I'll play it for you..." and in his cockney-based-yankee-flavoured-yard-spiced accent, Ollie went on to explain that he was getting good response to the record, which he had mixed and produced. He planned on getting copies pressed and sold.

Though he was more into the current techno-drum-'n'-bass-orientated scene, Mo was interested. Over the years he'd known Ollie, Mo had always encouraged him in his musical pursuits.

Mo's fate, in the shape of a frosty, dark pint of Guinness, caught up with him.

Ollie laughed. "Them man will kill you with drink, trust me! You know how much times I leave here mash up?"

They talked, working on their drinks as they kept coming. Halfway though his fourth pint, Mo realised he'd never make it. He looked across at Bertie, whose eyes he could hardly see any more. Peter and Oswald were singing "Breaking Up is Hard to Do" out of time with the Alton Ellis classic booming through the now crowded pub. Junior was having a close conversation with a buxom woman at the bar. Mr Kline and Lester still sat pretty steadily in front of their rum glasses.

For the third time, Mo got up and visited the gents. Each time he felt less and less steady on his feet, which was no big thing, since no one else in the place seemed to be either. He relieved his bladder, then washed his hands and splashed cold water on his face. Drying up with his kerchief, Mo carefully observed his reflection in the scratched mirror on the wall. He felt quite shook up, but he found that he liked the state. After the emotional hurts of the past week, being half-drunk felt good.

He went back to the table, back to the other half-pint of his Guinness.

"It's your last night as a bachelor, rude boy... you might as well get wrecked!"

Ollie laughed as he slipped back into third gear to overtake an irritatingly slow van. The Celica sprang forward like a leopard; two motions on the steering wheel and they were gassing freely down Commercial Road. The breeze through the window licked against Mo's face, tickling his senses out of the liquor-induced state he was in. He was thanking God for Ollie, for saving him from that band of roughnecks! The invitation to come along to the early gig Ollie was doing in a South London spot had been... heaven-sent.

Mo felt a little better now, back in control. One thing he was remembering about stout: you drink it for hours and feel mild; but when it holds you... it holds you! Beside him Ollie, who had managed three pints of beer in the short time he had spent at the pub, was happily drawing on a spliff he had pulled out of his pocket as they drove off. He had offered some to Mo, who had had to decline his offer to "take a draw, man". Ollie was big built and trained by years of heavy raving...

All the same, Mo was happy to go out. He hadn't been anywhere since his return and tonight — especially tonight — he was going to enjoy it. His head didn't hurt any more, the bad feeling in his stomach had gone. Later, he would take care of... later; for now, he was going to free his mind and party.

The way Ollie was driving, it didn't take them long to get there. From the front door down, you had to push your way inside towards the bar. A second room, a darker one at the back, wasn't as crowded. Ollie had joined two other DJs in the control booth, where they took turns in serving a diet of rare groove and swing, with just a slice of jungle for the hungry ravers.

Girls of all specifications were there, and though Mo wasn't dressed too slick tonight, he could feel one or two possible "plays" hanging his way. But he took his juice and moved next door, where the bass was slower and the lights lower, thinking how good it was that reggae music had come full circle back to culture in the space of a couple of years.

Mo nodded to the remixed Luciano tune, slipping through the crowd towards the back wall. It felt good being in the vibe, one more body swaying to the beat, heartbeat to heartbeat. Mo felt better now than he had when he left the pub; though the place was hot, the large fans helped to keep it bearable.

The two young men spinning the plates knew their job. Now and then they sent dedications to girls in the audience or passing celebrities, publicising one of the main community radio stations out of South London. The mood around Mo was right, relaxed and mellow. Everything was everything...

Mo finished rocking to Coco Tea's *Holy Mount Zion* before easing out to go look for Ollie, buy him another beer. As he stepped out of the crowd and turned the corner of the bar, he almost bumped someone coming the other way. Instantly he recognised the scowl and the medallion, and frowned with displeasure.

"We meet again!" Raymond nodded as if they were old friends. Right behind him, Mo saw without undue surprise the bulky figure of Paolo, waving to someone across the room. Paolo, with his suit and open shirt, looking like some Cuban pimp. Paolo, with his satisfied face, probably high the way his eyes were squinting. Paolo, with two goons at his back scanning around like they were mean dudes bodyguarding some VIP...

"Hey, the groom! How things, Mo?"

Paolo smiled a fat, two-faced smile. Right away that upset Mo. He felt like Paolo knew something and was laughing at him. Frowning, he said, "Things were cool until now..."

He surprised himself with his hostile tone of voice. Maybe it was to do with the drinking earlier on, or maybe Raymond's hyena-like smile was too close.

Paolo, oblivious to Mo's visibly unfriendly face, slapped him on the shoulder, still smiling. "Come and have a drink! What you having?"

This man was the last person Mo wanted to have a drink with. He was trying not to sound too aggressive, but something was stirring slowly inside him. "I got some move to make. Some other time..." he said firmly.

But Raymond was still in his face. Nobody had moved yet except Paolo, who smoked his cigarette and took time to gaze at a passing girl's shapely rump.

"My brother says he wants to have a drink with you," Raymond hissed too close to Mo's hear. Their eyes locked and Mo felt a very strong urge to hit him in the teeth, real hard.

He heard Paolo say amiably, "Come on, Mo. Let me buy you a drink, for good luck..."

That was what did it. This guy was making fun of him! Mo was certain now that Paolo was taking him for a fool. He really thought he was going to get paid! Though he would have preferred to deal with the matter another time and in another place, Mo was now too annoyed to wait. Behind Paolo, he recognised the man who'd been in the car that afternoon, and the other big-built guy with the shaven head and the glasses, a local boxing celebrity, light heavyweight (until a dependence on "chemical substances" had put paid to his career). Fitzroy's bodyguard until his employer's untimely demise, he now did the same job for Paolo. It was, after all, a family business...

Mo looked straight at Paolo and nodded. "OK."

They stood at the bar, Raymond hovering not too far away so he could still hear, the two "boys" taking up space a couple of yards away behind Paolo. The crew got their beers.

"To your health!" Paolo lifted his glass to Mo.

Mo took up his glass. "And to yours too," he said, unsmiling. He drank some juice. He felt in no way intimidated by who Palo was tonight; he didn't even care how many goons he had with him. Righteous anger does that to you. Without anyone to watch his back, Mo was ready to say things that needed to be said — right there.

"So, you're ready for the big day, huh?" Paolo smiled again amicably.

Mo made a face, took another sip from his glass. He thought about something Pearl had said. After a few seconds, he leaned a little towards Paolo. "Look — I wanted to tell you: I don't know what happened to that money you was talking about..." He thought he saw a little glint in Paolo's eyes at the mention of money. "...But I found out about who robbed my jewellery shop..."

Whether Paolo understood what he meant, Mo couldn't tell; his face didn't show anything. "Yeah?" he asked, like he was really interested.

"Yeah." Mo nodded slowly.

They were eye-to-eye, "feeling" each other, and Mo knew that Paolo didn't think much of him.

"What's that got to do with it?" Paolo asked.

Mo looked into the crowd for a short few seconds. One thing he didn't like was to be taken for an idiot. In this particular case, the insult was even more biting. Yet he refrained from involving Paolo directly. "I know it was Fitzroy, OK?"

Paolo was good at putting on faces; maybe he could have made it as an actor after all, a B-series one... "What you talking about?" he asked.

Mo wondered whether to do it, reasoning that he wouldn't be putting her at risk. "I talked to Pearl the other day..." he said casually.

Paolo wasn't smiling any more. No, he seemed annoyed now, not in such a good mood as he had been. He spelled out what was on his mind drily: "Listen, Mo. Why Pearl tell you that is her business. But like I said, this was business money. So forget about Fitzroy..." To Mo's surprise he signed himself like he had before. "You owe me what your brother took, right?" To make his point clear he stated, "I'm sending my people to collect from next month." Then he lit a cigarette with the studied manner of someone who thinks himself powerful. After all, he was the notorious Paolo Sousay, big on the scene and with a reputation that spoke for itself.

But he didn't know Moses Aldridge, because he said, "You don't wanna fuck with me..." Then

149

he straightened up, ready to move off; his drink with Mo was over.

That last remark got Mo real cold. He said, "You talk about thirty-five grand... I lost nearly fifty worth of merchandise. Call it even."

The look Paolo threw him would have intimidated most people who knew the man. "Even?" he repeated. "Have the fucking money ready — if you love your life."

This was a direct threat, and one coming from a man who was rumoured to have chopped off a man's hand in a dispute over money. But Mo's hurt and pain had translated into anger, a cold fury rising from inside. He was being played for a fool, and that was never a good thing to do to him, no matter who the offender was! The dangerous temper he had managed to curb only through years of practising the martial arts was still there. As a youngster, he would always run from fights — until some kid went too far and pushed him beyond the edge. Then Mo had got mad, and that was always bad news. Tonight he was feeling the fire still there, seething in the pit of his stomach, but he could still hold it down... just about.

Until Raymond got involved. He had overheard the last exchange and decided to exalt himself. He stepped up to Mo, close up once again, and leered at him. "You ready to die, boy?"

Mo didn't do it consciously, and only those close to them saw it. Raymond sure didn't expect it. But the hard blow from Mo's forehead hit him right on the bridge of the nose. He yelled in pain and fell back into a group of unsuspecting young women who screamed when they saw the blood on his face. Suddenly people backed away from around them and there was the sound of breaking glass.

Paolo hadn't moved, shocked by the speed of Mo's reaction. And Mo wasn't running either; he just took a stance and waited for Paolo's two thugs — who had just realised what had happened and were rushing his way. He knew the bouncers had searched everyone at the door — so there shouldn't be any gun play...

The tall man got there first, and walked straight into Mo's right foot. He doubled back, winded, as the kick sank into his stomach. Mo would have struck him again, but the ex-light heavyweight was on to him now, a furious look on his dark face. His mistake was to try to take off his glasses, which wasted a precious second of his time. The man was too strong to fight at close quarters, and too tall to hit on the head, so Mo slid forward quickly, shot his right foot into the advancing boxer's knee, then, with the same leg, kicked him in the groin area. The combination was too much to bear. The big man screamed first, then bent over and dropped to his knees, holding his crotch.

The whole action didn't last more than a minute. The music had stopped and the DJ was saying something about "peace".

Mo backed up against the bar. Paolo had slipped further away from him, watching but not trying to get to him; he was too big and too slow to fight nowadays. Mo breathed deeply, willing the breath to spread deep through his stomach region. He emptied his mind. This was one of the very few real fights in his life — and it was a big one. But he felt no panic. Just like his teacher used to tell him, the system was taking over. Mo found he wasn't planning his moves, only reacting to what was coming, hitting hard and fast, and accurately. He wasn't thinking about losing either, no matter the numbers... Focused, oblivious to anything around but the enemy, he waited.

The tall soldier was rushing in again, holding something in his elevated right hand. His face was contorted with anger, he shouted an invective and the hand came down fast towards Mo's face. Mo parried instinctively, but felt something hard cut into his forearm. He delivered a hard blow to the man's face, doubled with a solid knee to his crotch. The soldier crashed to the floor.

That was when Mo saw Raymond coming back. The head-butt had stunned him for a while, but now there was a mad look in his eyes and blood over his face. In his left hand, Mo spotted

152

the shiny blade. Swearing, Raymond came rushing, but he was holding the knife too high to be a professional. All the same, Mo forced himself to relax and waited, surprised to feel no fear at all. He started to move away from the straight line of attack at the last moment, dodging to his right because the tall soldier was getting up from the floor again to the left. Raymond didn't toy with him. He slashed downwards to catch Mo's face, so Mo had to take a half-step back to angle his body out of line. He grabbed Raymond's left hand and twisted it hard while hitting the elbow. Out of balance, Raymond bent forward, and Mo slammed the sole of his right foot down on his knee. The perfect move... There were two sharp, almost simultaneous cracks, as both joints dislocated. Raymond yelled and dropped to the floor like a discarded puppet. He wouldn't be any more trouble...

Mo could see the tall soldier had grabbed one of the bar stools and was ready for a third try. He edged a little away from the bar, sidestepping. Something made him want to glance back — and that's when he felt like the ceiling was crashing on top of his skull. He fell to his knees as a kick crashed into his ribs. Blood was dripping on to the side of his face, but Mo tried hard to stay conscious; he had to get back up or he was dead. Someone else seemed to be trying to kick him as well. He felt a blow to his mouth and it went numb very quickly. Then something hit him on the forehead, and he couldn't see much after that...

But his will to survive was stronger than the pain. "Get up! Get up!" a little voice was whispering in his head.

He heard someone say: "Leave him to me!"

It sounded like Paolo's voice.

That dog, Paolo, who had treacherously hit him on the head from behind...

Mo was getting angry again and that made him get back up on his feet. His arms were trying to parry the blows instinctively, as he couldn't see much for the blood over face. His right eye was closed. The kicks and punches kept coming. He was trying to step back, get some breathing space, but hands were grabbing and pulling at him. He was aware of people screaming, but no one seemed to be helping. So Mo gathered the little energy left in his battered body and rose up from his bent-over posture with one mighty push of his arms, literally diving forward to the floor and rolling on himself in an attempt to gain even a second's advantage on his attackers so he could stand up straight again.

All the time he was thinking that someone might just pick up Raymond's knife and use it...

Two kicks rained down on his back. Then he heard a shout, followed by a cry of pain. He raised himself on one knee and lifted up his bruised face. He could just see someone making space around him and he realised that he wasn't being kicked any more, so he got up shakily.

What he saw made him feel good: a man with his back to him hitting the tall soldier full force with one of the barstools. The tall guy fell down, stayed down. Then the man, dressed in white, raised the stool again and swung it into the boxer's body, hitting him across the ribs. That bent the ex-contender in half and he stepped quickly out of range of another imminent swing.

Mo could see Paolo now, back against the bar, his hands held out like he wanted to talk. Two more men had joined the one in white, one on each side of him: one short, brown and stocky with a dark shirt, and the other in yellow and black. Mo felt in his pocket for his kerchief, wiped his face as best he could. He could see the two bouncers now, the ones from the gates... no, three of them! Where had they been when he was being beaten up? Now they were playing tough, but the three men didn't seem to be the kind to beat upon. The man with the dark shirt said something loud to one of the bouncers, but Mo found he couldn't hear properly on his left side. He shook his head, which made him feel dizzy.

The man in white turned and looked at him. "You all right, Mo?" he asked.

Though he was in terrible pain, Mo was stunned. His right eye was closed, but the left one told him this was no mirage he was seeing. "Lucky?" he mouthed, incredulous, feeling pain in his jaw as he tried to talk. He couldn't believe it. It was Lucky! Mean-looking, bigger than the last time he had seen him. Mo didn't usually believe in luck but here he was, owing his life and limbs to the incredibly timely appearance of Lucky himself!

His friends had no weapons, but they had closed down on Paolo. Suddenly he didn't seem so hard any more.

Lucky looked Mo in the face, asked, "You can walk?"

Mo nodded. He legs were the only part of his body that didn't hurt.

Lucky turned and took a few steps towards Paolo. He pointed menacingly. "Anyweh I see you in South London again I kill your pussyclaat, yuh ah hear me?"

Paolo's face looked like he was not well. He wasn't so stylish any more, with his boys piled up on one side like so many beaten dogs.

Lucky came back to Mo. "Come, Mo," he said. He led the way out. His two friends took time to stare at Paolo some more before following them.

Through his pain, Mo pointed at Paolo as he was passing him. "You hit me from the back, you motherfucker!" It didn't sound like much, but he felt he had to say it anyway. He followed Lucky through the watchful crowd and into the main room.

A shocked Ollie came up to him. "Mo — what happened, man? You all right?" He seemed really worried.

Mo forced a smile and nodded, then walked on until he felt the mellow breeze outside.

Mo remembered watching a television programme years before, in which people had talked about having "near-death" experiences and how they felt afterwards. He knew now what they meant. His body wasn't so much paining him as feeling... absent. Curiously he felt numb all over, though he knew the pain would come later.

The dashboard clock read eleven forty-eight. Lucky's car radio played low. In the back, his friends debated freely on the best strategy to "take out" Paolo Sousay...

"We shoulda take him away and kill him tonight," the shorter one with the dark shirt said.

His companion disagreed. "No, man. Dem move deh fe plan... No witnesses," he explained.

"Dat pussy rob my cousin couple years back. Me nah forget him, you know!" the short man, whom Lucky had called Archie, said firmly.

Lucky turned from his driving towards the back seat. "Hey, Bing, you know seh is him bredda gi' me up to the police dem time deh?"

"Enh!"

"Yeah, man. Is inside I find out," Lucky added bitterly. "Fe dem whole family ah informer dem, from time. Ah dat make me leave my area."

Bing didn't like that at all.

Lucky said, "Archie, you know seh ah Sammy bredda this?"

Archie pushed his head over to look at Mo. "Fe real?" he asked.

Mo nodded.

"Respeck, Papa!" Archie offered his closed fist to Mo, who hit it but not too hard. He was starting to hurt all over now.

Archie seemed genuinely glad to meet Sammy's brother. He told Mo. "Sammy ah one wicked youth. Respeck due!"

Bing said from the back, "Dat man could sing, man, trust me!"

Lucky said to Mo, "Is God alone make me reach dat place tonight, you know, Mo! Is only because Archie supposed to meet one gal in deh," he added with a smile. "I never know it was you fighting."

Archie said, "Me see the fight start just when I get inside... You good, man!"

Mo managed a little smile. He was good. That was true — else he'd be dead by now...

Lucky said to his friends, "Here wha' happen: better ouno forward to the base and deal with the business. I gwan take care ah my man here and reach later, seen?"

158

He dropped Archie and Bing in Peckham to get their car, then drove out towards Sydenham at good speed.

He glanced at Mo's face. "How you feel?"

Mo nodded slowly. He was all right, considering. His head was busted in at least two places, his right eye shut, his mouth swollen, and there was a cut in his left arm... not to mention the aches all over his body. But he felt this pervasive satisfaction to have taken on three men and caused them at least as much pain as he felt himself. Raymond, for one, wouldn't be going to any dances for a while...

"Is when you come back?" Lucky asked him.

"About three months..."

Mo didn't sound too good. Lucky asked again, "Is why you was fighting dem boys about?"

Mo looked at him sideways (even his neck was causing him pain now). Here was the man he had wanted to talk to all along, the only one who might tell him about Sam's moves before he died. He understood now why Lucky hadn't been around — he'd moved to south London. Mo said slowly through his swollen top lip, "Paolo, he said Sam took thirty-five grand from them... He wanted me to pay back..." He saw the blank expression on Lucky's face. "What happened?" he asked.

Lucky took time to think about it, then he told Mo: "Mek I tell you somet'ing, Mo: if I'd ha' been out dem time deh, Sammy wouldn't be dead..."

Mo simply looked at him, waited.

"Is me and Sammy get busted, through dat same boy set we up, seen? We get nine months because the lawyer get we off two ah the charges, but I beat up some battyman in deh, so dem gimme some more time..." Lucky stopped at a red light, turned to Mo. "I tell Sammy seh fe wait till I come out to go deal with the boy. I call him from prison one night and him tell me seh 'im a go deal with the matter himself. All me ah talk to him, him seh it personal now, and him ah go kill the boy... You know how Sammy cyant t'ink straight when him get mad!" A pause. "One week later him was dead..." Lucky's face was set, his eyes hard on the road through the windscreen. "Sammy was my bredda, you know, Mo... I'd ha' lay down my life for him."

Mo knew Lucky was speaking from the heart. From the very first week the then ten-year-old Lucky had landed on their estate from his native Jamaica, he and Sam had been like twin souls. Sam was a crazy kid in the first place, and in Lucky he had found the ideal partner. Lucky was tough and cunning. Mo had seen him get into fights in his first year at school and had been amazed at the fearless disposition of the short youngster. Lucky would take on twelve- and thirteen-year-olds and, though he hadn't always ended up on top, you could bet that same kid would somehow sustain a grievous injury a few days later. Sammy would lick his wounds and lay

160

in wait for the offender with a piece of stick, never letting a beating go unavenged, so that after a while he'd got himself a reputation as a "nutter", as they used to say in the area — someone best left alone. By the time they were fifteen, Mo had found out that Lucky and Sammy got paid "fees" by local white boys for helping them in neighbourhood teenage gang fights...

Mo wanted to know something. "Tell me, Lucky... Sam was paro when he went after Fitzroy...?"

This time Lucky turned away from the road long enough to look him square in the face. "You ah hear me, Mo," he said firmly, "me and Sammy got off that shit almost a year before that... before we go prison. We did business, yes, but we never lick it again."

Mo asked, "Who told Sam it was Fitzroy who robbed my shop?"

Lucky's surprise was genuine. "Fitzroy?"

"I only found out this week," Mo told him.

Lucky had a thought to himself for a moment, before he said meaningfully, "I glad Sammy killed him raas!" He nodded. "Dat's why him seh it was personal!"

Mo couldn't bring himself to tell Lucky the whole story just now. Had Sam found out about the real set-up but not got to tell his partner somehow? Through Mo's throbbing head, that question kept coming up.

Lucky swerved into a street on the right and stopped the car further down. Mo looked up at the two-storey house as he painfully stepped out of the car. His body ached badly but his mouth hurt the most.

"So this is where you are now..."

Lucky switched on his alarm and led the way past the low iron gate. "Yeah, man," he said, pushing his key into the lock.

Lucky sat Mo in a round chair and gave his wounds a critical look. The room was spacious and uncluttered. Three large potted coconut trees formed a green triangle right in the middle of the Mexican rug.

Mo winced with pain as Lucky passed one finger over the gash above his eyebrow.

"You need some stitches, you know, Mo... The other one's all right. Just a bump."

The other one — where that fat swine Paolo had hit him — must have swollen pretty big now. Strangely for the circumstances, Mo recalled Aunt Alda telling Sam quite a few times how the family was renowned for its tough skulls, something of that order...

Mo wanted to have a look at himself in the mirror. "Where's the bathroom?"

"Come."

He followed Lucky upstairs, taking his time to ascend. The reflection in the mirror wasn't encouraging, and Mo had a last angry thought for those cowards back there. The trail of dried blood from his forehead ran past his swollen upper lip, staining his trimmed beard like dark mud. On the other side, his eyelids were puffed like a man who'd just lost a title fight. He'd never been a vain man, but what he saw in front of him could have done all right on screen as a stuntman's make-up. The irony was that he had looked so good after his haircut earlier that afternoon! He wasn't concerned about the gash on his left arm. Lucky had said it was "just a scratch", and he sure knew a lot about wounds...

"You better get washed, then we can see better wha' ah gwan," Lucky told Mo.

Just then there was the sound of a door opening nearby. Mo turned from the mirror and looked at Lucky. Quiet steps on the carpet...

The woman who had just stopped short at the bathroom door gave vent to her shock at the sight of him. "Oh my God! Lucky, what happened?" she cried out, her hands raised to her face.

Mo was staring with his one good eye at the woman, who wore a long green T-shirt as a nightdress. She took two horrified steps forward, but stopped when Lucky said, "It's Mo."

Mo had not expected this. He hadn't seen Lucky's sister since she'd gone to university in faraway Leeds, years ago. He tried to say her name, but it came out different.

Arnette was squinting as she slowly approached, searching his face for what had been features. "Mo?" she said, looking at Lucky, then back at the injured face in front of the sink. When she had finally recognised him, it seemed even more shocking to her. "What happened to you, Mo? You need to go to the hospital!" she declared.

Lucky told her, "Cool, man. Him all right. Help him wash him face."

Arnette took a clean rag and ran some warm water for Mo. She kept looking his way, surprised to see him after so long and shocked to witness his terrible state. As she cleaned him up with as much care as possible, she started asking her brother questions until he briefly filled her in. She dressed Mo's injuries, patched him up as best she could, remarking that he should have stitches to the eyebrow cut. Mo said no, it would be OK; he was already feeling a little better. Arnette spread some balm over his bruised ribs — nothing seemed broken, fortunately — and sat him down comfortably in the living room while she made some tea.

"So, you all right now, sah?" Lucky smiled as Mo sipped his hot drink as best he could.

Mo nodded. "You saved my life back there."

Lucky didn't need to answer that.

"Why were you fighting, Mo?" Arnette asked. "You never used to fight..."

That was true. Back when they were growing up on the estate, Sam was always the one to fight, rarely Mo. Lucky had neatly omitted to mention what the fight was about or who he was fighting with, so Mo saw no point in involving Arnette in such matters. Most of all, Mo didn't want to bring up his brother's name — not first anyway: he knew Arnette would get to the subject of Sam sooner or later. She had been his closest female friend and confidante back in their early years, before she left the area for university at eighteen.

So Mo sidestepped. "I didn't pick the fight... It's just one of those things. When did you get back to London?"

"About four years ago now."

Lucky got up. "Mo, I have certain moves to make. Wait till I come back, seen? Granny gwan look after you..."

Mo recalled that Lucky usually referred to his younger sister as "Granny", had always done so, on account of her father always repeating that that was who she looked like. Arnette had always had the same face, it appeared, born looking like an old person as some babies are. She was pretty enough all the same, with a short nose, a high forehead, and rich, bronze-coloured skin. Though she had never liked her nickname, she'd got used to it eventually.

So Lucky left and Arnette was looking at Mo like she used to: very penetratingly, as though expecting to discover his mind simply by staring. For him, seeing her again took him back so many years, to the happy, carefree days of childhood.

He told her, "It's really good to see you."

She smiled from the low couch where she sat. "I knew you would come back. I always knew."

"You look the same, Arnette. You don't get old."

"You look like big man now, though!" she told him.

Arnette, unlike her brother, had managed to lose some of her accent through exposure to academic circles. Yet she would naturally slip back into it when mingling with her own people.

"So, you finished university?" Mo asked her.

"Yes. I have a degree... but no job."

"It's hard, I know..."

They talked a little, of anodyne things, but Mo's mind wasn't on that. Though he was talking to Arnette, she seemed distracted by something. It was as if she was there in body alone while her thoughts were somewhere else.

Mo had drunk most of the tea and his head felt a little clearer now. Arnette straightened herself on the couch and said, "Look, Mo, I have something I want to tell you... but I'm finding it hard."

Mo said, "Arnette, you're like my sister; you can always tell me anything, you know that!"

She had been like the sister he and Sam never had. But right now her hands were clasped together and she seemed... embarrassed. Mo had never seen her like this before. Even after such a long and taxing day, his brain could still click on

166

to something strange. He suddenly knew what he had picked upon earlier, but couldn't pinpoint...

"You know I can't lie, Mo. But... this is the hardest thing I ever had to do."

Mo asked what was on his mind: "You said you came back to London four years ago?"

Arnette looked deep into his face and nodded slowly.

"You saw Sam..."

Mo wasn't really asking her, but she nodded slowly again, still staring at him.

The word "When?", which he had on his lips, didn't get to be formulated, because Arnette said very softly, "The last night..."

Another series of blows from his foes couldn't have rocked Mo's head any more than what he had just heard. He shook his head, incredulous. "Sam was with you?"

Arnette nodded very slowly.

In Mo's mind, the links were connecting together. He took a full minute to ask the next question: "What did he say?" Mo felt the emotion rising as he looked at the last person to have seen his brother alive — apart from his killer. Arnette! He was shocked, astonished that fate, nothing less, had led him to this house tonight.

He saw Arnette look down for a moment before she spoke: "I'm going to tell you everything I know, but I want to ask you one question first."

Mo nodded, waiting.

"Did Lucky tell you why Sammy shot Fitzroy?"

"Lucky didn't know it was Fitzroy who robbed me until I told him tonight."

He was surprised to hear Arnette say, "That wasn't the reason, Mo. Sam would have robbed him, but not killed him..."

Mo told her, "Fitzroy tried to fight him, right?"

To reconstruct Sam's last day didn't feel good to Mo, but after the turmoil of the last few weeks searching for the truth, at least he was about to know.

Arnette was still stalling.

"Arnette, I have to know," Mo said very seriously. Bitterly, he added, "That was what the fight was about tonight, because I don't know for sure what happened."

Arnette's face opened up. "Who did this to you?" she asked.

Mo sighed. He realised she knew more than him anyway, so why hold back...? "I had a fight with Fitzroy's brothers," he said. "They're trying to make me pay for what Sam took from them."

Arnette got up from the couch, tears welling in her eyes as she came across to throw her arms around Mo. He held her despite the pain he felt, and rocked her gently as she cried. It seemed as if she hadn't yet cried for Sam, and her tears came down, wetting Mo's face as he stroked her hair gently. He let the grief pour itself out of her, feeling emotional too but holding back.

When Arnette settled down a little while after, she took his hand in hers and told him what he couldn't have guessed.

About a year before the tragedy, Sam and Lucky had turned up at Arnette's place in Leeds one afternoon. She had been in infrequent contact with her older brother, due to his slide into drugs. Though she loved him dearly and had helped him as she could all through his troubled years, she'd virtually turned her back on him when she saw she couldn't get him to quit drugs.

As for Sam, the deep love she'd had for him as a youngster had made it even worse. She was angry at Lucky but deeply vexed at Sam.

So that day she had been taken totally by surprise, but the two looked in a bad way. They told her they had problems and needed a little break from London. Not that hard-hearted after all, Arnette had found them a place to "catch" for a few days. That was when she managed to convince them that their habit was about to destroy both of them and, to her surprise, they swore to quit and straighten up their lives. Arnette wanted to believe their promises.

They'd gone back to London eventually, and the next call she got from them was from a remand centre. But they assured her, both of them, that the promise still stood — and as she visited them during the next few months, Arnette had seen that her brother and Sam were looking better. By the time Sam came out, Arnette had moved to London.

Then she told Mo, in a roundabout way at first, something that was another major shock for him that night, something he had to ask confirmation of twice to believe.

"You... and Sam!"

Arnette smiled almost shyly.

Mo asked again: "But how? Why?"

Never in his wildest dreams could he have imagined that Arnette would end up with Sam — never. They had been so close, like brother and sister. The more he recalled their relationship growing up, the more astonishing it sounded. Arnette, who used to get girlfriends for his philandering brother... Arnette, who was so hard with boys that no one in the area had managed to get even a little break with her... Mo recalled her tactics of discouraging the advances of any suitor, no matter how genuine, with a coarse "Look, you're not getting nothing, all right?"... Arnette and Sam? That was unbelievable.

"He changed in prison," Arnette insisted. "He didn't like it, but he cleaned up in there. When he got out, he came to stay by me and it just... started from there..."

Mo took a minute to digest this. "So he wasn't hooked no more when he went for Fitzroy?"

Arnette shook her head silently. Mo waited, but she'd stopped talking, so he asked her, "Did Sam find out about Julia?"

He saw Arnette tense up. "Who told you?" she asked.

"I've only found out last week... Did Sam know, Arnette?"

She simply nodded. There was a silence, as if both were guessing just how much the other one knew.

"Who told him?" he asked. "Fitzroy?" Mo realised it was the first time he had considered that option. Surprisingly, it seemed to explain everything — well, almost.

"That's why Sam shot him," Arnette said calmly.

"What?"

"Fitzroy told him about him and Julia, he lost respect, so Sam got angry... He said he hadn't meant to kill him even then, but Fitzroy tried to grab his gun."

It was personal, Sam had told Lucky... Mo imagined his brother's anger at Fitzroy's revelation. Then he hit upon something. "But... who told Sam it was Fitzroy who robbed me?"

Arnette knew the answer to that, and Mo knew that she knew, because he realised now that Sam had told her things he had kept even from Lucky. Maybe he'd been feeling too embarrassed for Mo to tell even his closest friend.

Arnette answered in a way that slowly chilled Mo's brain: "There's only one person at the centre of all this, Mo. Think..."

171

The thought came to him quickly enough, and he cringed as he said, "Julia..."

He saw confirmation in the stillness of Arnette's features.

"Julia?" he repeated, his mind racing through the facts.

Arnette wasn't moving. But she sighed deeply and told him, her hand still around his wrist, "It's an ugly story, Mo; everybody is guilty... except you." She paused, then fixed him with her piercing eyes. "Do you understand what I am saying to you? Everybody is guilty, except you..."

He didn't quite get it, still feeling stupid not to have made the connection about Julia. He asked, "But why did she tell Sam? She set up the robbery, she must have known he would tell me..."

"She was blackmailing him."

"Yeah, I know," Mo said sombrely. "I met Fitzroy's wife, she told me the story."

Arnette bit her lips and sighed deeply. "Sammy... She was blackmailing him too."

Mo looked at Arnette blankly for a moment. What was she talking about? It couldn't come out of her mouth, it seemed. She kept looking at Mo, then glanced away, then down.

He was getting lost in the conjectures in his mind. "Why? What are you saying?"

Then Arnette talked, all at once, looking at Mo only intermittently until she had spilled it all out. Mo listened, feeling his heart sinking in his chest as the cruel words penetrated his head. As if tortured from delivering the awful secret she had harboured for all these years, Arnette was almost shaking as she spoke.

Sammy had been haunted by the shame and remorse of his betrayal for over ten years; it had eaten him from within, and eventually he had died from it. His last night on earth had been spent shaking and crying, torn asunder by guilt. Arnette told Mo like she had heard it from Sam: how he had fallen victim to Julia's wicked devices one night while wrestling with his addiction. Sam had not denied his guilt, Arnette said, but had never managed to face his brother with the truth. The fear of losing forever Mo's love was too much for him. That last night, on the run for his life, he had begged Arnette to ask Mo to forgive him, fearing he wouldn't see his brother again. She had tried to reassure him, to soothe his broken heart. But Sam had been right; the next morning he'd tried to shoot his way out of the police ambush, and had died there, shot dead on a North London street. Arnette said that he'd vowed they wouldn't take him alive. And he managed to take one of the police officers with him...

"I done Mo wrong..." That's what Sam had told Angie on the phone that night.

Mo was too stunned to say anything. Now he understood. He felt Arnette's arms close around him, holding him tight. Through his daze, he heard her say, "Sammy left some of the money with us."

Mo stared at her. Money was the last thing he cared about right now. He felt physically sick in his stomach.

"He gave Lucky ten, and ten to me..." Arnette told him, adding, "I saved most of it."

So it was true after all... Paolo's fat smile came flashing in Mo's mind. Sammy had still managed to take care of his people in his last desperate hour.

Arnette was still holding Mo as she said, somewhat lower, as if ashamed to speak it out, "You must know who kept the rest of the money..."

To Mo it was like the twisting of the blade already plunged into the depth of his soul.

Arnette had new tears rising again in sad eyes. "He'd left the money with her for you when you came back, but he realised she wasn't going to give it to you..." She cried silently. "I told him to forget it, but he wouldn't listen to me, Mo..." Arnette was reliving the last hours with Sam, and it was clear she couldn't take it. She wiped her tearful face, but the water just kept coming. "He called her in the morning. She was supposed to meet him..." She was sobbing like a little girl now. "The police were waiting for him..."

The horror rested in the unstated, the unbearable implication of what Arnette had just said. Mo couldn't tell when the tears had started, but now he found himself weeping, crying like he had never cried before, crying like almost every big man cries at least once in his lifetime when sorrow tears his soul apart. And his breaking down only made Arnette's pain deeper. They held each other, not letting go, like shipwrecked survivors on a raft, lost on the deep, dark ocean. Their world uprooted and their dreams drowned for ever, Arnette and Mo clung to each other for what seemed a very long time, digging deep inside their collective golden memories to find something pure, something unspoilt, to hold on to.

After what seemed like hours, Arnette got up and led Mo through the corridor towards the back bedroom. Slowly opening the door, she took his hand and pointed in the semi-darkness at the bed against the wall.

"She'll be three in December," she whispered into Mo's ear.

• F A I T H F U L L Y •

27 September 1996
Toronto

Dear Nicole,

I *hope these words will find you in the best of*
health, also Vinny. Maybe you'll be surprised to read
this letter, maybe you've been expecting it. In any
case, it took me a few weeks to write it. I have been
settling down slowly here in Toronto. The weather is
still good right now, but I'm not going to enjoy the
winter when it comes. I hope school's going well and
that you're working hard. Your grandmother here
with me says you must be first in the class and Vinny
also! She says she was always first when she was at
school...

I *miss you and I have been wanting to write you*
from... well, from when I left. I hope you will not be
angry with me for leaving you so suddenly, at least I
hope you're not any more. If you are I can't blame you.
Although you're still a young girl, you can probably
guess it took something very bad for me to leave. The

hardest thing for a father, I found out, is not to be able to tell his child the truth...

Nicole, I really love you, I want you to know that, and the three years I spent away were never happy because I was missing you. Certain things are not easy to put down on paper, for me anyway. But I'm a musician and maybe some day I can write a song that will explain to you all I'm feeling now. I'm going to try and get back to my work here for now. You know your grandmother's health hasn't been good these last few years and she is happy to have me look after her. I know you will soon be able to come and see me; all the family here asks about you.

I want you to be strong for me, I need to know you will make me proud in everything you do, just as I have tried to make you proud in my life. Nicole, maybe you won't believe me because I know you are eager to grow up fast and become an adult, do what you like doing, be free... but you are now living the best time of your life so don't rush, please. I am your father and I should know a lot more than you, but I'm not wise. The only thing I can tell you is that respect is all that matters in this life. The rest never lasts... Respect yourself always, so that you will always be able to face your conscience.

I am asking you to take care of your brother for me. I know he will need me more than you, but until I can guide him, please try your best to help him. I know he has his ways but boys don't grow as fast as girls so he still needs a little time. He's your blood, and you and him are the most precious things I have.

I want to tell you that you have a cousin... a little three-year-old girl, very pretty. Her name is Aminah, which means "faithful". She's your uncle Sam's daughter. I hope I can arrange for you to meet her soon.

Please phone Aunt Alda from time to time to see if she's all right. Try to go with her to the cemetery sometimes. I hope you will be able to write, and Vinny also. He will ask you questions you cannot answer right now, but tell him I love him and I won't forget him.

I leave you now, praying God will keep both of you safe. Be good and work hard. Remember: do good always, and good will follow you. And don't be sad, for everything is just for a while.

Love always,
Your father,

Mo

Books with ATTITUDE

THE RAGGA & THE ROYAL by Monica Grant Streetwise Leroy Massop and The Princess of Wales get it together in this light-hearted romp. £5.99

JAMAICA INC. by Tony Sewell Jamaican Prime Minister, David Cooper, is shot down as he addresses the crowd at a reggae 'peace' concert. Who pulled the trigger and why? £5.99

LICK SHOT by Peter Kalu A black detective in an all white police force! £5.99

PROFESSOR X by Peter Kalu When a black American radical visits the UK to expose a major corruption scandal, only a black cop can save him from the assassin's bullet. £5.99

SINGLE BLACK FEMALE by Yvette Richards Three career women end up sharing a house together and discover they all share the same problem-MEN! £5.99

MOSS SIDE MASSIVE by Karline Smith Manchester drugs gangs battle it out. £5.99

OPP by Naomi King How deep does friendship go when you fancy your best friend's man? Find out in this hot bestseller! £5.99

COP KILLER by Donald Gorgon When his mother is shot dead by the police, Lloyd Baker goes for revenge. Controversial but compulsive reading.£4.99

BABY FATHER/ BABY FATHER 2 by Patrick Augustus Four men come to terms with parenthood in this smash hit and its sequel. £5.99

WHEN A MAN LOVES A WOMAN by Patrick Augustus The greatest romance story ever...probably. £5.99

WICKED IN BED by Sheri Campbell Michael Hughes believes in 'loving and leaving 'em' when it comes to women. But if you play with fire you're gonna get burnt! £5.99

FETISH by Victor Headley The acclaimed author of 'Yardie', 'Excess', and 'Yush!' serves another gripping thriller where appearances can be very deceiving! £5.99

UPTOWN HEADS by R.K. Byers Hanging with the homeboys and homegirls in uptown New York. A superb, vibrant novel about the black American male. £5.99

GAMES MEN PLAY by Michael Maynard What do the men get up to when their women aren't around? A novel about black men behaving outrageously! £5.99

DANCEHALL by Anton Marks. Reggae deejay Simba Ranking meets an uptown woman. He thinks everything is level vibes, until her husband finds out. £5.99

BABY MOTHER by Andrea Taylor. Life really is full of little surprises! £6.99

OBEAH by Colin Moone Mysterious murders and family feuds in rural Jamaica, where truth is stranger than fiction. *Winner of Xpress Yourself '95 writing competition!* £5.99

AVAILABLE FROM WH SMITH AND ALL GOOD BOOKSHOPS

Out on the streets, they call this murder...

"For the Streetwize, the Wanna-Get-Wize & the Otherwize™"

The UK's best black and urban culture Internet mag-e-zine, seen! This artical webzine drops it crucially from street level with X-amount of irreverent style. Internet Underground calls it: "a hip, ultra-cool cultural trip through music, fashion, pop culture, art, society and politics."

Published monthly, but updated weekly, YUSH is accessed daily by many thousands of global readers with attitude. It leaves a memorable impression on those who have seen it. But, don't take our word for it:-

"Promisingly provocative slang-filled laid back black culture zine in a bonafide ruff neck style. YUSH Ponline mashes up British, Afro-American and Jamaican opinion and polemic with a more relaxed sideways review of black art and culture."
INTERNET

"YUSH Ponline is ideal for the clued-up and those who want to be filled in...By no means exclusive to black culture."
.NET

"Hip, current, and smart, YUSH Ponline is a must-read for anybody interested in urban, African-American culture."
NETGUIDE

"A rare British success story."
THE WEB

Check out the latest issue for yourself at
HTTP://WWW.YUSH.COM

FOR SALES, AD OR OTHER ENQUIRIES CONTACT MICHAEL CONALLY AT
SNAIL MAIL: P O BOX 3680, BRENT, LONDON, NW6 5BL, UK
E-MAIL 1: YUSH@YUSH.COM • E-MAIL 2: YUSH@DIRCON.CO.UK
TELEPHONE: +44 (0) 181-930-7000 • FAX: +44 (0) 181-933-4839